An Unforgettable December

I0727256

An Unforgettable December

The Unforgettable Series #7

Nikki A Lamers

www.ingramcontent.com/pod-product-compliance
Lightning Source LLC
Chambersburg PA
CBHW040233170726
48295CB00014B/908

* 9 7 8 1 9 5 0 2 7 2 3 3 4 *

Copyright

This is a work of fiction. Any names, characters, events, incidents, businesses, places are either the product of the author's imagination or used in a fictitious manner. Any resemblance to actual events, locales, or persons, living or dead is purely coincidental.

Text Copyright © 2024 Nikki A Lamers, Nicole Mullaney
All Rights Reserved

No part of this book may be reproduced or transmitted in any form or by any means, electronic or mechanical, including photocopying, recording, or by any information and retrieval systems, without the written permission of the publisher, except where permitted by law.

Cover Design by Frey Dreams

Frey Dreams

ISBNs: 978-1-951185-29-9 ebook
978-1-951185-28-2 paperback

Chapter 1

Dean

"Need some oil?"

I glance at the guy out of the corner of my eye, making sure he's talking to me before shaking my head. "No thanks."

"It helps you look better on camera," he adds, quirking his eyebrow.

"Don't need it." I run my hand through my inky black hair, wondering for the fifteenth time how the fuck I ended up getting manipulated into being here. Every guy around the room is dressed, or half-dressed in some kind of Christmas theme. There's a Jack Frost across the room, a snow king, Santa wearing red briefs and a hat, a bunch of elves at various levels of fucked-up, someone I assume is Scrooge, another in a red tux without a shirt underneath who could be Santa or Scrooge and a guy painted green. The Grinch is great, but seriously? And me, I'm wearing red Santa pants with black suspenders and boots, my chest bare.

He shakes his head and huffs a laugh. "Suit yourself."

My phone vibrates in my pocket and I pull it out, one of my best friends lighting up the screen, the guy who's responsible for me being here. Swiping the screen to answer, I accuse, "How the fuck could you do this to me, Joe?"

His laugh echoes through the line. "Who was I supposed to send? Christian? While Bree is home with the baby? She would kill me."

"What about you?"

"My sister is on the crew! No way in hell I'm getting half naked in front of her, no matter how good the cause."

"Isn't she only a year younger than you?"

"Yeah, she's twenty-six. So, what. That has nothing to do with it. She's still my little sister."

"I'm sure there was someone else you could've asked."

"Sure, there is, but you owe me and it's easy for you to take off work."

I groan in frustration. "Yeah, yeah." I owe him a lot – both him and Christian. They're always there, no matter how much I fuck up. They've been my best friends since our freshman year of college and they've seen me at my best and my worst. Christian is now married with a kid, and Joe just started dating someone new, so they haven't been around as much, but I know they would be if I needed them. Just like I'll still do anything for both of them. That won't ever change. It's why I'm here.

So, suck it up Dean.

"How's it going anyway?"

"It's like being in the locker room at the North Pole." I'm unsure how else to describe it.

He laughs. "Have fun but be good – it really is for a good cause."

"And what is that again?"

"You each represent a different cause throughout the month of December on their social media for an end of year push. The program goes all year and there has already been tons of marketing done for the fundraiser, but this is for a last-minute add-on product they'll share at the fundraiser event they want you at on Thursday night."

"Next Thursday? That's fast."

"It is, but this is specifically for another push for everyone. They're working with non-profits for the homeless, terminally ill, a separate one for sick kids, food for the hungry, gifts for the holidays for kids and families, clothes, school, and office supplies for those in need, military families, families suffering from domestic abuse and a few others."

How can I back out on something like that? No way! I heave a sigh. "Fine. I'll deal."

"Stay away from her, Dean."

"Who?"

He huffs a laugh. "My sister, asshole. She's been warned about you for years, so she wouldn't touch you with a ten-foot pole."

"Why does everybody think I'm such a player?"

He ignores my question, believing the answer is obvious. "You know I appreciate you. Seriously, thank you for doing this." I grunt in acknowledgment. "I gotta' go. I'll catch up with you later."

"Sure asshole." I disconnect the call and slide my phone back in my pocket.

In the next instant, a hand slips into my pocket and pulls out my phone. Swiftly, I spin around in protest. "Hey!" A petite blonde with her hair pulled back in a French braid drops my phone into a black and red bag and slings it over her shoulder as she puts her hand up halting my movements. "That's my phone."

"No phones allowed on set."

I smirk. "On set?"

She rolls her grey eyes. Taking a step back she pushes a pair of brown glasses up her nose and slowly assesses me from head to toe. Pulling a bottle out of her bag, she squeezes something into her hand and mumbles under her breath, "You need oil."

Gesturing behind me, I begin, "I already told…" I gasp as her hands start rubbing my chest, sending a shock right through me. Clearing my throat, I attempt to do what I do best. "If you wanted to touch, all you had to is ask."

She laughs, her eyes dancing as she glances up at me from underneath her long eyelashes, a splash of freckles over the bridge of her nose bouncing as she laughs quietly. "Nice try, Santa."

I flash her an innocent smile as she steps back with a shake of her head. "This isn't me trying, beautiful." The guy behind me laughs, but I ignore him, my eyes remaining glued to her.

Stepping up to me, she tilts her head back, looking up at me as she licks her lips. I tilt my head down to hear her better, my dick jumping. "Something to keep in mind when it comes to me…" she begins.

"Yes?"

"Those lines don't work on me." She pushes the bottle of oil into my chest, pushing me back, her lips twitching in amusement. "You can finish that yourself or ask one of the guys for help, just don't miss anything."

"Wait, what?"

"Make sure you get your back too." She smirks, taking another step away from me. "You'll get your phone back after you're done." She spins on her heel and walks away, her hips swinging.

My eyes remain glued to her perfect ass as she impossibly disappears in a room full of men. Damn.

Heaving a sigh, I glance down at the bottle in my hand. Is she kidding? My eyes shift to my half-oiled chest. I guess not. She didn't even flinch. Relenting, I do what I'm told, rubbing a little on my arms, and grabbing a towel to wipe my hands.

"Dean Chambers."

"That's me." There's no turning back now.

Chapter 2

Leah

"Today went really well," Scarlett states as she pushes her long, wavy, red hair over her shoulder. "It's almost worth missing out on Black Friday shopping."

I huff a laugh setting down a box of our Christmas decorations on top of another box before sitting on the opposite end of our oversized tan couch that barely fits in our living room. "You just think that because you got to do the makeup for a lot of guys."

She grins. "Not just guys, hot men! I think my favorite were the ones that needed oil rubbed all over their muscles."

My face heats almost instantly, my fingers trembling at the reminder. Dean fucking Chambers. He hasn't changed a bit. Remembering his abs, my mouth waters making me admit to myself that's not exactly true. What the hell was my brother thinking sending him? I guess it makes sense. It's probably not his first modeling job with that lean, firm body, strong jaw, blue eyes that make you melt without even trying and a killer smile, but I don't like it. He's trouble.

"Oh, what are you blushing for, girl? Did I miss something?"

Of course, Scarlett would notice. She hasn't only been my best friend since middle school, she's been my roommate for over eight years. We've been through every breakup, every success, and every failure together. No one knows me better. I heave a sigh. "Well, you know when Davis backed out at the last minute because he heard I went on a date with Beau?"

"I still can't believe that jealous idiot."

"Whatever." I roll my eyes. "Anyway, I called my brother for help and he asked one of his friends to do him a favor to help me out."

"Oh, was that the guy I saw you rubbing down?"

"I was not rubbing him down."

She bursts out laughing. "Oh, yes you were and he was hot."

"Yeah, but he's a bad idea."

"Why?"

I grimace. "He's a player."

"Joe told you that?" She arches her eyebrows in challenge.

"Yeah, but it's not like he's making the stories up. He lived with the guy all through college and a couple years after."

"He can't be all bad. This event you're doing is for a good cause, or technically a lot of good causes."

"It's my job!"

"A job that you fought for and a Christmas fundraiser you pushed for, planned everything and have been working your ass off for to boost donations before the holidays. A lot of people are going to benefit because of you.”

A smile tugs at my lips knowing all the good this will do. “No.” I shake my head. “It’s because of everyone who’s been working hard to get it done in time for Christmas and the people willing to donate their time and money for the causes. I’m just doing something I believe in. Besides, I want to do a good job to prove my worth. I’ve been there for over three years now but this is the first big project they’ve allowed me to run. I’m so nervous about everything falling into place. I need it to go well.”

I bite my lower lip, running my teeth over it in thought. She’s right, but Joe said he was going to call in a favor to help me out. If it wasn’t for Davis quitting on me at the last second, I wouldn’t have been so screwed, but I don’t have time to look for another December 5th and there are not a lot of men around here that fit what we need. The printer already says we’re way behind, but it’s the last thing on the list besides last-minute details for the event. I’m not about to let it all fall apart now.

“It will go well and you have plenty of time. You need to take a break so you don’t burn out before you turn thirty.”

“So, I have time.” I shrug and she narrows her eyes at me. My lips twitch in amusement knowing she’s about to react. “Well, I am only twenty-six. That can be my New Year’s resolution.”

She plants her hands on her hips and narrows her eyes. “What am I going to do with you,” she mutters shaking her head.

"Maybe we should invite some of the guys from the shoot today over to help us decorate our place for Christmas. We are busy and could use the help. It would be fun," she suggests making me laugh.

"Those guys are not coming here to decorate our house for Christmas."

"Well, they could come for other things." She wiggles her eyebrows suggestively.

I burst out laughing. "Scar, stop."

Smirking, she waves it off. "In the meantime, it's the weekend and you can't do anything for the next couple days, so we're going out for a drink." She jumps up, tugging on my arm.

"Hey!" I argue, knowing it's pointless.

"Quit whining. You need a break! And you owe me."

"Fine," I groan, letting her tug me towards the door. "At least let me put on some shoes."

"Whatever," she huffs in mock annoyance.

I tug on my black city boots sitting by our front door and glance in the mirror, quickly, dusting my nose with powder, and applying some mascara and lipstick as she waits, watching. "Where are we going, anyway?" I ask, slipping my ID and phone in my back pocket.

She loops her arm through mine as we walk out the front door. "Not far. We need to be able to walk home together later."

"That's not an answer." She laughs. "Scar!"

"A few of the guys were talking about going out to that restaurant that turns into a dance club at night."

"The guys? Like the guys from the shoot today?" My eyebrows hit my hairline.

"Of course."

"I thought you were joking about inviting them over."

"Well, I kinda was, but I'm not joking about hanging out with them tonight."

"I'm not dressed to go out for something like that."

Sighing, she halts her footsteps, staring at me. "Yeah, you are. You look hot in those jeans."

"But I'm wearing a button down. I look like I'm ready to go to work."

"So, get creative. Unbutton it and show off your lacy black Cami underneath."

"It's almost winter in Maine!"

"Almost is nothing like the real thing and you know it will get hot inside. Roll up your sleeves, tie the bottom in a knot and take it off when you're hot. You need this or I might strangle you before the event."

"Gee, thanks," I grumble, deadpan. With a heavy sigh, I fix my shirt so I look more like I'm ready to go out, even with my hair pulled back. "I know I've been stressing about this, but I need it to go well. It's not just that I want to prove myself. So many people are depending on these funds. I don't want to disappoint anyone."

"It will go amazing knowing you, but not if you don't destress."

"You're probably right."

She grins, picking up her pace. "You know I am."

Chapter 3

Leah

It's not long before we walk into the already crowded bar. The license plates from all over the world plaster the left wall, interspersed with Christmas decorations, likely wherever they fit. It makes me wonder if they used to be on cars, or if they had them made. To the right is a long oak bar lined with garland wrapped with red lights, the same decorations framing the back of the bar with an eighteen-inch porcelain tree centered among the liquor bottles. Hanging in the back of the club is a large wreath with colored lights the tables were removed to make up a dance floor. It's small but it works.

Scarlett weaves us expertly through the sea of bodies towards the bar, ordering us both a lemon vodka and soda. "Here," she offers moments later.

"Thanks."

"Cheers!" She grins holding up her glass and we both take a drink.

"Hey, it's makeup girl and wonder girl!" a deep voice proclaims as he throws his arms over both our shoulders, almost making me spill my drink. "Oops, sorry." He gives me an apologetic smile.

"Wonder girl?" I arch my eyebrow at the familiar guy with brown hair and eyes. He shrugs giving me a look I'm sure he's used before to get what he wants. "David right?"

"She remembers me!" He grins, his arm dropping from Scarlett.

"Well, we did just see you a couple hours ago." She smirks.

"Glad you guys made it. Can I buy you both a drink?" We laugh, holding up our drinks and toast one another again. "Next round."

Scarlett leans in by my ear, reminding me, "Try to relax."

"I'm here, aren't I?"

She laughs, looking around. "Oh, Ben is here. I'm going to go say hi. You're good here, right?" she asks and spins on her heel without giving me a chance to respond. Glancing back at me, she winks.

I flip her off and take a sip of my drink, already starting to warm up from all the body heat in here. I look up at David his arm still draped over my shoulders and ask, "So, have you done a lot of modeling?"

His eyes light up as he begins to ramble. "Not a lot, but I've done a few jobs. You may have seen me in the ads for the department store? They wanted me…"

The cacophony of voices and music filling the small space drown out his voice. I take the time to look around searching for other familiar faces. Scar's right it's hot in here. I slide out from underneath his arm and slip out of my shirt, tying it around my waist as he turns to the bar and orders another drink.

I spot some of the other models from today and some of the crew along with the younger staff from my company Charming Affiliate Marketing. Thankfully the senior staff doesn't appear to be here, so I'm comfortable enjoying the night. The room definitely has more women than men. I'm surprised by how dressed up everyone seems to be too, hinting that someone shared there would be models here tonight.

My gaze lands on a girl a couple feet from me with long, dark hair wearing a short, tight, black dress with spaghetti straps and two-inch platforms. Why would you wear that to go out to a random bar in Maine this time of year anyway? Maybe she heard the model rumor.

She pushes into the guy standing in front of her and presses her lips to his. The guy's hands reach around her, one tangling into her hair and the other cupping her ass, pulling her into him while she pushes closer, not caring that her dress has nowhere to go. My eyes widen as they start making out, not giving a damn who's surrounding them. His lips move to the crook of her neck a flop of black hair falling over his face making me gasp.

Is it him? No way. "Dean fucking Chambers," I mutter under my breath. I should've known.

Ripping his lips away from her skin, his steel blue eyes crash into mine with a spark of surprise. I gasp, realizing I said that much louder than I thought. Damn. A lump forms in my throat and my stomach twists. I hate that just a look from him has my body reacting, especially when he just had his tongue down another woman's throat.

"Wonder girl." He grins as he pulls away from the woman, pushing her back as she glares at both of us.

My heart begins to thrash against my ribcage, my eyes glued to his. This man. Shit, I'm in trouble.

Chapter 4

Dean

The moment my name leaves her lips, I know it's her before I look. "Wonder girl." I grin as I mumble the name I've been hearing out of the guys mouths all damn day wondering how she'll react. She pinches her full lips, attempting to hide behind her drink as she takes a sip. She's heard the name, but she doesn't appear to know why. Interesting.

She looks hot as fuck in a lacy black tank, accenting her ivory skin. I take a step closer to her as the woman who just threw herself at me latches onto my arm, trying to claim me, but that shit doesn't work with me. "Dean," she whines, "I thought we were busy."

"Nah, I'm good. I'm talking to Wonder girl." She huffs as I disentangle my arm without looking in her direction.

She steps into my space again and wonder girl rolls her eyes dramatically. "Are you really that desperate?"

I huff a laugh before I can stop myself. The woman glares at her. "How dare you! Who the hell do you think you are?"

"There's plenty of other models here. Is he really worth getting hit over?" She challenges, ignoring her question. I'm not sure if I should be pissed at the insult or turned on.

"Screw you both," the woman mutters as she spins on her heel and stalks away.

I laugh and step closer again. She smirks as she takes a step back looking up at me from underneath her long eyelashes, her eyes swirling with blue and green. "Thanks for the save."

"Didn't look like you really wanted it."

"Like you said, she's obviously here to hook up…"

"With a model," she interrupts.

"You know that's not my actual job, right?" I quirk a brow, for some reason needing her to know I'm more than my face. "I'm just here helping out a friend."

"And taking advantage of the benefits."

"Hey, is it my fault women throw themselves at me?" She may be right, but the words coming out of her mouth feel like a punch to the gut. Let alone, I let that woman kiss me hoping to get this firecracker out of my damn head. Her walking into this bar ripped that idea to shreds.

She gives me a look and opens her mouth, probably to call me on my shit, when David steps up to her and drops his arm around her shoulders, making me stiffen. He's one of the assholes who made that fucking bet. She glances up at him, her body not folding into his like I've seen other women do all night. Thank fuck. He lightly swirls a drink hanging it over her shoulder. "I got you another drink, Wonder girl."

"Thanks." She glances at her still half-full glass and downs it. My jaw drops as she sets the empty glass on the bar and changes the subject as she takes the drink from him. "And why does everyone keep calling me that?"

"We saw how hard you were working all day," David claims, telling her a partial truth.

"Well, thanks," she murmurs, accepting his response as she takes a sip of the drink he just handed her.

I clear my throat, refusing to walk away while this douchebag is anywhere near her. "It's nice to see you taking a break."

"You sound like my roommate."

"Your roommate?" I arch my eyebrow in question.

"Yeah, I need to go find her. I'll see you guys later!" She dips out from under David's arm and I breathe a sigh of relief. My gaze drops to her ass and back up as she waves over her shoulder.

Moments later, she hip checks a petite redhead and her arms go up in the air as they dance. I'm not able to take my eyes off her. Damn I could watch her move all night. My dick jumps in anticipation of something I already know he can't have. David groans beside me reminding me he still has his eyes on her along with other assholes in this room. For some stupid reason that just pisses me off.

"Maybe she's not as much of an ice queen as we thought," David comments.

I narrow my eyes on him. "She just has fucking standards."

He laughs. "Or maybe she's just a bitch and needed some loosening up."

"What the fuck?!" I shove him in the shoulder and he stumbles back, wide-eyed.

"Dude?!" he grunts, holding his hands up in surrender. "Don't be such an asshole."

"Treat her with some fucking respect!"

He smirks; the look making my stomach roil. "I'll happily fucking worship her."

Without thought I grab him by the shirt and shove him up against the bar, glaring at him. "What the fuck did you just say?"

"Hey, assholes," the bartender yells instantly right behind David, "settle the fuck down or get the hell out!"

My eyes narrow on David, his hands up as if he's innocent and his lips twitching in amusement. He's trying to piss me off. "Watch yourself," I warn before I release him with an extra shove and step back, stalking towards the dance floor to find her.

Chapter 5

Leah

I make my way through the crowd, finding Scarlett talking to her cousin, Ben. I hip check Scar and grin up at him. "Hi Ben. You're here."

"Hey, Leah! Good to see you." He leans down, giving me a hug.

"Of course, he is, I wasn't lying about that. His boyfriend is one of the models."

"Really? Who's your boyfriend?"

"Jacob." He grins.

"He's so nice and hot too."

"Yes, he is."

"So why did you leave David? He looked like he wanted to eat you for dinner."

I scrunch my nose up in disgust. "Exactly. He was giving me creep vibes and he's way into himself."

"That sucks." Scar frowns. A new song comes on and she jumps. "Oh, I love this song! Let's dance!"

I nod and finish my drink setting it down on a table behind them, the alcohol suddenly hitting me hard. I guess it has been a long time since I've let loose. My hips begin to sway and I raise my arms in the air, closing my eyes as I get lost in the music.

A firm hand falls to my hip as a warm front presses against my back, moving along with me. I try to pull away, but I feel sluggish, so I lean my head back and look up, finding another face or two that I recognize as one of the guys I worked with today, but I can't remember his name.

"You can really move," he tells me.

"Thanks," I mumble my throat suddenly dry. The room starts to spin, so I stop.

"Are you okay?" Scarlett steps in front of me, but I can't focus on her moving form.

"Um, yeah." I gulp and tap the hand gripping my hip hard, desperate to get away and breathe. "I think I just need water and I'm going to the bathroom."

"Okay, I'll come with you."

"No, I'm okay, I'll be right back." I look towards the back corner, keeping my focus on my destination, rushing towards the bathroom.

As I push through the door, the room spins and I stumble to the sink. I plant my hands on each side of the sink, taking a couple deep breaths, trying to calm my stomach and stop the dizzy spell. Desperate for a reprieve, I splash my face with cool water.

The door swings opens as someone walks in. I lift my head, glancing in the mirror and gasp as David catches my gaze in the reflection. "You're in the wrong bathroom," I mumble, my words slurring.

"No, I came looking for you. I heard you might need some help."

I shake my head, my movements wobbly. "No."

"Are you okay, wonder girl?" His voice sounds anything but sincere. "You don't look so good." He takes a step towards me. I try to step away, but I fall back against the wall of the bathroom stall. "Just relax. Let me help you," he urges, planting his hands on the wall, next to my head, closing me in.

He runs his finger under the strap of my Cami, making me feel naked. "No, no, no," I mutter as a prayer.

The door hits the wall with a bang, but my limbs are either too weak or too slow to react. "Get the fuck away from her!" Dean's voice echoes against the walls.

"I heard her calling for help," David claims, stepping away.

"Dean," I murmur, gasping for breath, relief consuming me.

"Asshole," Dean grunts as everything suddenly goes peacefully black.

Chapter 6

Dean

Grateful the police are gone and I got my statement over with, I slide down the wall next to my bed and sit on the floor with my knees propped. My hand runs down my face to the back of my neck, rubbing it as I stretch, trying to release the tension. I haven't slept on the floor like this since college, but there was no way in hell I was leaving her side. She looks so beautiful, peaceful, as I watch her chest rising and falling methodically in sleep. My old black Imagine Dragons concert t-shirt looks sexy as hell on her, along with knowing she's wearing a pair of my boxer shorts underneath the dark gray sheets covering her legs.

She begins to stir. I shove myself off the floor and lean against the wall as her eyes flutter open. She groans and wipes her eyes looking around the room. "How are you feeling?" I ask gently.

Her head snaps to me and she winces from the movement before her eyes go wide. "Dean?"

I pinch my lips tightly together and give her a stiff nod. Does she not remember? Shit. "There's some water and aspirin on the nightstand if you need it," I offer, attempting to give her time to process.

She reaches over, downing the aspirin and the entire glass of water. "Why does my mouth feel like I ate sand? And why am I here? What happened?"

Heaving a sigh, I drop down onto the edge of my bed, looking at her anxiously. This is not something I want to tell her. I was hoping she would remember. She looks back at me, her blue-green eyes lighter, more vulnerable, hitting me hard as they begin to narrow. "You don't remember anything?"

She shakes her head pulling her knees up to her chest, the sheet going with her like a shield. "Not really, we didn't...um…"

"No!" I insist with a hard shake of my head. I don't want her to think the worst of me.

Her eyes suddenly widen in fear and she gasps, pulling the sheet even tighter around herself. "David…he…he…" she stammers, not able to get the words out.

"He didn't do anything. Well, that's not exactly true, but he didn't touch you. I got there before anything happened."

Tears spill down her cheeks and she looks away, staring out the window. "I'm so fucking stupid!"

I inch closer, not wanting to startle her. "No, you're not. It's not your fault."

"I took a drink from him. Just because I was working with that asshole for a day doesn't mean I know anything about him. I know better than to take a drink from anyone. How could I be so stupid?"

"Stop. You were surrounded by people you knew. Why wouldn't you trust that you were safe?" I just want to make her feel better.

Her gaze swings back to me. "There's two rules I've always been taught to follow to protect myself when going out. Don't go anywhere alone and don't ever take a drink from anyone you don't know really fucking well. Apparently I broke both those rules."

I reach up and wipe the tears from her cheeks, no longer able to hold back. "It's not your fault he's an asshole."

"What happened to him?"

"I don't exactly know. I wanted you out of there and the police don't tell you anything."

"The police?"

Yeah, they were here early this morning to take my statement. I didn't tell them you were sleeping in the next room because I didn't want to wake you. But he won't come near you again."

"How do you know?"

"I hit him and left him with the bouncer, telling them he put something in your drink."

Her eyes widen and she reaches for my hand, tingles shooting straight up my arm as she runs her fingers over my cracked and bruised knuckles. "Which is why the police were here. Thank you," she murmurs without meeting my gaze.

"You don't have to thank me."

"Why am I here, Dean? Why didn't you just bring me home?"

"I was going to bring you home, but you passed out in the Uber before you could tell me or the driver where you live and I guess your roommate figured you'd tell me. I wasn't about to take you back in there to ask."

She nods. As she looks up, meeting my gaze, my chest tightens at the range of emotions passing through her teary gaze; fear, gratitude, relief, and heat. "Thank you."

Not able to stop myself, I reach up and cradle her face in my hands, wiping her tears with my thumbs. "I'm just glad I was there."

A soft whimper escapes her lips before she presses them to mine taking me by surprise. But I don't waste a second and kiss her back. My lips move in a slow rhythm over her soft full ones. She moans, the sound sending heat throughout my body, my dick jumping in excitement. My tongue juts out, wanting a taste but she pulls back, denying me. "I'm sorry, I shouldn't have done that."

I quirk a brow, hoping she doesn't regret our sweet kiss that felt anything but.

"After last night, my mouth just tastes gross."

Relief floods me. "There's an extra toothbrush under the bathroom sink if you want it."

"Thanks." She scoots to the edge of the bed before looking back at me, her cheeks flushed. "Um, my clothes?"

I give her an apologetic smile. "You threw up on your jeans and tank, so I threw them in the wash for you. You still have your bra and panties on, but I thought you'd appreciate something to wear."

Her face turns brighter with each word I utter. "Um, thanks?" She squeaks as more of a question, making me chuckle.

"Don't worry, I didn't look more than I had to. Not that I didn't want to." I don't want her to think I'm not interested.

She clears her throat, changing the subject. "So, Scarlett knows I left with you?"

"Your roommate?" She nods. "Yeah, she knows. Although, you might want to call or text to let her know you're okay."

"She knows I'm safe with you."

My eyebrows draw down in confusion. "Why would she know that?"

Her puzzlement matches mine. "Because you're Dean. I'm sure Joe asked you to watch out for me." Her gaze drops to the floor as my heart plummets.

"Joe?" I ask as reality slams into me. "You're little."

"What?"

"I used to call you *little* Leah."

She grimaces. "He's barely a year older than me. I've just always been small."

"Fuck," I mumble under my breath. "I knew you were working there, but I didn't expect you to be all grown up."

"Wait. You didn't know I was Joe's sister?" she asks, incredulous.

"It's been a long time since I've seen you." I know it's a weak excuse. I'm such a fucking idiot. I said I would watch out for her, but I didn't realize she looked like this.

She huffs and pushes off the bed, stalking into the bathroom without another word. "Fuck." I run my hand through my hair in frustration. "I'm sorry, Leah!" Without a response, I sigh heavily, trudging towards the kitchen to make us both breakfast and get some much-needed coffee. Little all grown up is hot as sin. I'm in so much trouble.

Chapter 7

Leah

My reflection glares back at me as I untangle my hair from yesterday's braid. I look like I got run over by Santa's sleigh taken over by rogue elves who then jumped out and danced to Jingle Bell Rock on my head. It's the same way I feel. I'm pissed at myself for being so stupid. Never again.

But Dean… I sigh, not knowing if I'm irate or relieved. He wasn't watching out for me because I'm Joe's little sister, but because he wanted to. I always knew he was a good guy, but he's also a player. It comes so naturally to him. He's charming. It felt like he was interested in me. That's what he does though, right?

Then again, maybe he wouldn't have kissed me back if he knew who I was. Maybe it's good he didn't know because that kiss... I couldn't stop myself with the way he was looking at me and what he did for me. But what now? I shake my head, shoving away my question. I'm thankful for him, no matter who he is to my brother.

I walk out of the bathroom, finding his bedroom empty. Grabbing my phone, I see a few missed calls and texts. Ignoring the others, I open one from Scar. "Are you okay? I'm worried!"

"I'm okay. Just woke up. Dean didn't have our address."

My phone beeps instantly with her response. "The police want to talk to you right away to take a statement."

I grimace, setting my phone back down as the smell of bacon hits my nose. "Mm," I murmur, following the scent. I walk towards the open living space, a combined, living, dining, and kitchen, the white granite countertop separating the kitchen from the rest. "Smells good." I drop onto a stool, leaning on the counter. "Is anything for me?"

He chuckles, the deep sound making my stomach flip. "I made you breakfast. Scrambled eggs, bacon, and toast. Is that okay?"

"That's sweet, Dean. Thank you!"

"No problem. I'm sure you need it," he mumbles, keeping his back to me.

He's right, I can't argue with that. I spin on my stool taking in the large Christmas tree sitting in front of a picture window, the branches bare of decorations or lights. "You have a Christmas tree."

"Of course, don't you?"

"Not yet. Thanksgiving was just two days ago. I've been too busy. When did you have time?"

He shrugs as he plates the food, setting one in front of me and another next to it. "I got it on Thanksgiving."

"What was open?"

He sits down next to me. "This is Maine, Christmas trees are everywhere." I arch my eyebrows and he laughs. "My parents have a ton of trees. I cut it down on their property."

"Now that makes sense." I nod, realizing I don't really know much about Dean besides what Joe has told me over the years. Most of Joe's stories constitute drinking, parties, women, bad decisions, or a combination. Then again, last time I saw him was probably their college graduation. He obviously didn't remember me. Maybe he's changed. The woman from last night flashes through my mind making me grimace. Maybe not.

"You don't like my cooking?"

I blush and shake my head as I finish chewing. "No, that's not it. I was just thinking about something."

"Something?"

"My brother."

"I can see how Joe could put that look on your face." He smirks, making me blush a deeper shade of red. "Or are you thinking about how he told you to stay away from me, warned you about me, told you I'm a player and then you woke up in my bed this morning?"

"What?" I gasp, wide-eyed.

He waves his hand like it's no big deal. "It's fine. Your brother has seen me at my best and my worst. But why don't you come to your own conclusions about me?"

"It's not like that."

He puts his fork down, his plate empty and focuses his full attention on me. "You sure about that?"

"When you mentioned your parents' property, I was thinking how I never knew that about you."

"So, you don't think I'm an asshole or a player?"

"No," I retort, my nose wrinkling without my consent. He laughs. "You're obviously a good guy."

He winces, standing he grabs his plate, moving towards the sink. "A good guy but a player."

"You did have your tongue down some random's throat when I saw you."

He barks out another laugh and turns, facing me. "So, since I'm such a good guy, why don't you spend the day with me."

"You don't want my company. I have a terrible hangover."

His shoulders slump. "I'm sorry that happened to you."

"I'm okay thanks to you. I just want to put it behind me. I will never be that stupid again."

"Are you going to the station to give your statement?"

"I guess I have to," I concede, my chest suddenly tight. "My roommate said they were at my place this morning."

He nods, striding towards me and putting his arm around me, rubbing soothing circles on my back. "Yeah. I can take you."

"That's okay. Scarlett will go with me."

He nods, pursing his lips. "Well, junk food and movies are a great cure for a hangover if you want to hang out later."

"Do you want to?"

"I'm asking, Leah."

I lick my lips. "I don't know…"

"Give me a chance to show you I'm not who you think and at the same time, I can help you forget about last night."

My heart squeezes. I don't know if this is a good idea, but when I look into his eyes, I can't say no. "Okay."

"Yes?"

"Yeah, I'll text you when I get home. Now, can I have my clothes?"

He laughs and kisses me on the top of the head, eliciting a gasp from my lips and tingles to shoot from my head to my toes. "Sure, but you look good in my shirt," he calls over his shoulder. My entire body heats as he turns to fetch my clothes. I watch, holding my breath until he disappears. Damn, that man...

Chapter 8

Dean

My hand remains poised above the door, ready to knock, but questioning everything about being here. This is Leah. She's not a woman I can just fool around with, but just because I'm here, doesn't mean anything will happen. I'm checking on her to make sure she's okay. I huff a laugh. Who the hell do I think I'm kidding? Yeah, I want to check on her, but I want something to happen. I can't fuck this up. Joe is too important to me. Maybe I should get to know her more to see if there could be something between us before…

The front door swings open. Leah's red-headed roommate stands in front of me, grinning like the Cheshire cat. "Are you going to stand there raising your hand all night or are you coming inside?"

A laugh escapes as I give her a crooked smile, attempting to act like she didn't catch me fighting with myself at their front door. "Hi, is Leah here?"

She nods and calls over her shoulder, "Leah, Saint Nick is here!"

Does she have a date tonight? "Um, I'm Dean."

She giggles and waves me off as she steps back. "I know who you are."

Leah stumbles into the room in light blue flannel pants with red and white Santa hats on them and a white tank with three red buttons between her breasts drawing my attention. She gasps as her gaze meets mine. "Oh, hi, Dean."

My smile falters. She doesn't seem very happy to see me, but at least she doesn't have a date if she's in pajamas...or maybe she does. "Hey, I thought we had plans for a Christmas movie night tonight, but I didn't hear from you..."

"I'm so sorry. I was exhausted after…" she pauses shaking her head.

"Well, if you're okay, I'm going to meet my brother and sisters for a drink." Scarlett stops and stares at Leah, waiting.

"I'm fine, Scar."

"In that case, don't wait up!" We remain silent as her roommate exits.

"I don't think I'd be good company tonight," Leah begins.

"I thought that was why we were going to watch Christmas movies."

She arches her eyebrows, her doubt obvious. "You, Dean Chambers, want to stay in on a Saturday night and watch movies with Joe's little sister?"

I flinch, quickly trying to hide it. "I want to stay in with you and do whatever the fuck you want as long as it will make you happy and help you forget about assholes and police stations."

She sighs, giving me a fake smile. "You don't have to do this."

"You're right, I don't." I step towards her until I'm in her space, looking into her eyes. This isn't about anyone but us.

Her breathing picks up its pace, becoming ragged before she suddenly clears her throat and takes a step back. "Okay, do you want something to eat or drink?"

I grin, holding up the bag in my hand. "I brought ingredients for Christmas corn."

Her eyes sparkle and she dives for the bag. "No, way! That's my favorite!"

I laugh. "I know. Your brother used to ask me to make extra for him so he could give it to you for Christmas."

Her mouth drops open. "He told me he made it himself." I shrug and she rolls her eyes.

"It's not hard; you just mix fresh popcorn with red and green chocolate candies and then drizzle it with melted white chocolate and either the red and green sugar or sprinkles while the chocolate is warm."

She reaches for my hand and tugs it, shooting sparks up my arm as she drags me towards the kitchen. "Well, let's go already!"

Dropping my hand, she pulls out a large bowl as I dump the contents of my bag on the counter. "So…"

She crosses her arms protectively over her chest. "Go ahead, get it over with and then we don't talk about it again. Agreed?"

"Yeah. How are you?"

Releasing a heavy sigh, she claims, "I'm fine. I'm tired, and felt like I had a hangover all day, but I'm fine." She puts the white chocolate in a microwavable bowl and pops it in the microwave. "The police station sucked. They don't think they have enough to press charges since I didn't go to the hospital and have a blood test to confirm what was in my system and there was no real proof that he put anything in my drink. I'm pretty sure the asshole got off with a warning."

"What?" My blood instantly boils as I drop the candy into the bowl, staring at her, mouth agape.

"Stand down, Saint Nick. I'm fine thanks to you."

"But…"

She shakes her head, turning her back to me and pulling the white chocolate out of the microwave. "I'm done talking about it." Ignoring me she drizzles the white chocolate over the popcorn.

I sigh and run my hand through my hair. She'll be pissed at me if I bring it up again and that's the last thing I want. I should've hit him harder. "So, what's with this Saint Nick shit?" I ask, attempting to appease her, but I'm not forgetting what that asshole did even for a moment.

She giggles, her shoulders relaxing as she grabs a giant spatula, mixing the popcorn. "One, you in your *25 Men of Christmas* outfit and two, you coming to my rescue."

The corners of my lips twitch up in amusement as we both pour colored sprinkles over the popcorn and stir. Stepping back, I lean against the counter, my finger tapping on my bottom lip as I rake my eyes up and down her body. "Well, I could always put on the outfit for you and do things to your body to show you I deserve that name."

Her face heats and her breathing quickens, giving me the desired effect. "Dean," her voice catches. With a shake of her head, she clears her throat and picks up the popcorn mixture, striding towards the living room. "You're definitely no saint."

I chuckle, following. "You got that right."

She sets the bowl on the coffee table and swipes the remote, flopping onto the couch. I sit next to her, draping my arm across the back of the couch and setting the bowl in my lap as she flips through a few movies. "What about Elf?"

"Sure." Laughter will do her good.

A smile tugs at her lips as she relaxes, leaning towards me and the popcorn mix, popping some in her mouth. "Mm," she moans, licking the melted chocolate off her fingers. My tongue juts out, my mouth watering. "This is so much better than I remember, but the chocolate is still a little melty."

My dick twitches and I clench my jaw. This will be harder than I thought. I fist a handful of popcorn and stuff it in my mouth, suddenly in desperate need of a distraction.

44

Chapter 9

Leah

Sunlight peeks through my closed lids making me groan in protest. Did I forget to close my blinds? I'm hot as hell and reach up to wipe the drool from my mouth when my pillow moves. My eyes flash open instantly, Dean's dark scruff inches from my face, his sweet musky scent filling my nostrils. I hold my breath, realizing I'm draped over his chest. I must've shifted when I fell asleep. What do I do?

He moans, shifting, his hand sliding to my ass. Reflexively, I arch into him, his morning wood pushing into my stomach, eliciting a gasp from my lips. "Leah?" Dean rumbles.

In a sudden panic, I push up and jump off the couch, my knee colliding with Dean. "Fuck!" He grunts, his knees pulling up as he covers himself, rolling onto the floor in pain.

"Oh, my God! I'm so sorry!" I can't believe I just did that! His face turns so red, it's nearly purple before it begins to lighten, while I incessantly apologize. When his breathing appears back to normal and he no longer looks like an exploding tomato, I approach tentatively. "I'm so sorry. Are you okay?"

"I'll let you know if I'm able to have kids one day." I wince. "It's a joke, Leah, I'll live."

"I'm sorry."

He exhales harshly and sits up, leaning against the couch. "Did I try to feel you up in my sleep or something?" he asks giving me his sexy crooked smile.

I laugh. "No, I just woke up. I guess you startled me."

He huffs a humorless laugh. "I'll have to remember not to scare the shit out of you if I want to protect my balls."

My face heats and I look away. "I'm sorry I fell asleep on you."

"I'm not. I'm just sorry with the way you woke me up."

It's so hot in here. Damn this man. "So, what are you doing today?" I ask, hoping the teasing stops before I decide to jump him.

"Spending the day with you."

My eyes fly back to his. "What?"

"I thought we were spending some time together and you were giving me a chance to show you I'm not who you think?"

"Yeah, but I have a lot of work to do for the event Thursday."

"Okay, how about I go home and shower so you can get some stuff done for work. Then I pick you up for pizza and finding you a Christmas tree later?"

"You don't have to do that."

"I know I don't." He stands and steps towards me, moving into my space. He holds my gaze before insisting, "I want to."

My heart skips a beat and I relent. "Okay."

He grins making my stomach twist. I bite my lower lip, holding back my groan. He wraps his arms around me, pulling me close. I smile, hugging him back and melting into his chest as if the spot were mine and mine alone. He kisses the top of my head and steps back. "I'm going to go before you change your mind. I'll text you when I'm on my way."

I wave as he walks out the door. My entire body sags as I exhale, collapsing onto the couch behind me. "Ugh! What am I doing?"

"Morning!" Scarlett announces making me squeal in surprise. "Sorry, didn't mean to scare you. I wasn't sure if that sexy man was still here with all the noise you two were making this morning and I didn't want to walk in on anything."

I shake my head and groan, trudging towards the kitchen to make coffee. "It's okay. Apparently I'm a little on edge this morning."

"Where's Dean?"

"He just left."

"You two seemed cozy when I walked in last night?"

"What am I doing Scar? I can't go there with him."

"Yes, you can!"

"But Joe…"

"Your brother doesn't own him and that man is obviously into you."

"But he's a player. I know I've gone out with a few different guys lately, but I don't sleep around. I like being in a relationship. I'm not the kind of girl who can act like sex isn't a big deal."

"I'm pretty sure with him, everything would be a big deal." She wiggles her eyebrows suggestively making me laugh. "And have you seen those hands? Can you imagine what he can do with those? And his tongue…"

"Stop!" I toss the kitchen towel at her and pick up a full mug of coffee from under the Keurig.

She laughs. "It will be worth it."

"Well, he's picking me up later for pizza and a Christmas tree."

She quirks her brow. "A Christmas tree?" I nod, my lips twitching. "You need to stop thinking so much. Have a little fun! He's hot and interested. Plus, you trust him. What could possibly go wrong?"

"Famous last words…"

Chapter 10

Dean

My nerves get the best of me, causing chaos to erupt deep in my gut. I wipe the counter down for the third time, needing everything to be perfect when she sees my place. I want her to like it. I've never been this concerned about a date before. Then again, I don't usually bring my dates to my house, or anywhere near my property. I probably couldn't call hookups a date either.

A knock sounds at the door as I throw out the paper towel in my hands, startling me. "Coming," I call, wondering who it could be. Striding towards the door, I yank it open, finding Joe on the other side. "Hey, Joe. What are you doing here?"

"Hey man. What do you mean? We were supposed to go grab a beer and watch the game. Did you forget?"

Groaning, I run my hand down my face in frustration at the reminder. "Oh, no. I'm sorry, Joe. I just didn't realize that was tonight. I've been really busy with work and other shit." Even I don't buy my lame ass excuse.

He arches his eyebrows in question. "Too busy to hang out? Well, we know it's not for a woman, so is everything okay?"

I flinch, a wave of regret slapping me in the face for my past. "Ah, yeah, everything is fine."

"Your parents?"

I shake my head. "No, I've just had a lot of shit going on, plus the favor you had me do for you is taking up more time than expected."

He winces. "I'm sorry. Thank you for that."

Shaking my head, I insist, "You don't have to thank me. I'm happy to do it. You know that. But I've been busy and I do have a date tonight," I concede, holding my breath as I watch his reaction.

He smirks. "That's what you're calling them now? Dates?"

"Fuck you." I retort, hurt, but trying not to show it, knowing that would've never bothered me in the past.

He chuckles and then halts, looking around my place, his eyes widening by the second. "Wait, you're bringing a date here?"

"Yeah, so?" I ask, my defensive undertones obvious. I pinch my lips tightly together, waiting for Joe's reaction, but he doesn't give me any indication he notices.

He arches his eyebrows in question. "So? You don't bring dates home. Your rule, not mine." As he takes in my space, a smile tugs at his lips. "Looks like you might actually like this girl. This place never looks this good for me."

Shrugging like it's no big deal, I chuckle, knowing he's right. "It's cleaning day," I claim, smirking.

He laughs. "Sure, it is. She must be pretty damn special if you're bringing her here on cleaning day."

"You have no idea," I mutter, wanting to tell him everything and at the same time knowing I can't, at least not yet.

His smile falls. "Wait, you're not planning to just seduce her are you?" I cross my arms over my chest, narrowing my eyes at him making him chuckle. "All right. So, what's your plan, Casanova?"

I grimace, hating the same nickname I used to flaunt, but quickly brush it off. "She needs a Christmas tree, so I was going to bring her here so we could walk the property and she can pick one out. Then we'll probably come back here and have pizza afterwards. Nothing too crazy."

"That sounds like a pretty good date. You're upping your game."

"Gee, thanks, asshole."

"Is she anyone I know?"

My eyes widen, not sure how to answer. I don't lie to him, but Leah would kill me if I told him. He'd probably hit me if I did and I'd deserve it. Fuck, what am I doing? "I'm, uh, not telling you who she is. I'm not even sure what the fuck this is at the moment."

He narrows his eyes, staring at me for a moment, trying to read me. "Huh, okay. Interesting."

"What do you mean by that?"

"Nothing. It just sounds like you actually like this woman. I'll look forward to hopefully hearing more about her."

My stomach twists. I want to tell him the truth, but what will he do when he finds out? I fucking hate this, but I have to take the chance. I've never wanted to be around a woman like I do her. She's worth the risk. "Yeah. Sorry about the beer and the game," I tell him, needing to move on.

"No problem, Dean. I'll catch you next time."

With a heavy sigh, I close the door behind him. Guilt eats at my insides, but I shove it down knowing Leah is waiting for me. I don't want to keep her waiting. My stomach suddenly churns in anticipation. I smile as I swipe my wallet and keys off the counter, excited to get to her and for the first time, bring a woman to my home.

Chapter 11

Leah

Dean pulls through a tall, wrought-iron gate, driving on a narrow drive into the woods. "I never took you for a serial killer," I mumble under my breath.

He bursts out laughing, the sound shooting tingles throughout my body. I glance at him out of the corner of my eye, his crooked smile remaining as he glances at the road ahead. "I did bring my ax." He gestures towards the back of his truck.

Narrowing my eyes, I glare at him, his responding chuckle making me impossibly hotter. Damn him. "Where are we?"

"My place."

"You live in the woods?"

"This is my parents' property. I have a house on the back of the property, far enough away from the main house."

"Huh. I didn't imagine you were one to live at home." He clenches his jaw, making my stomach churn. "I'm not judging, just surprised."

He relaxes slightly. "Well, it's not like they're ever here and they have over three-hundred acres."

My eyes widen in surprise as I taken in the stretch of pine all around me. "Why wouldn't they want to be here? It's so beautiful!"

He shrugs. "Yeah, it is and this is only a small piece of it. I always said one day I'd build my own house around here, but it's just me. Why leave when I'm already alone?"

"Dean…"

He shakes his head. "I didn't say that to make you feel sorry for me, Leah. My parents have another place in Colorado, New York, California, and England, but this is where I want to be."

"Oh, wow. I had no idea."

"Most people don't unless I grew up with them or they know my parents. Joe and Christian know, but they also know I don't like to talk about it."

"Can I ask why?"

He parks the car in front of a small cedar house, turns it off and twists his body to look at me. "For starters, my parents are assholes."

"I'm sorry."

He waves me off, like it's no big deal. "Don't be. It is what it is."

My heart squeezes, but I bite my bottom lip, attempting to hold back my reaction. "And your other reasons?"

"What?"

"You said for starters, meaning that's not the only reason."

"I did." He sighs. "The simplest explanation is people change when there's money involved. I've learned who my real friends are over the years."

"I'm sorry," I murmur, my heart breaking for him, making me want to curl up in his lap and comfort him, but I don't.

"Stop apologizing. It's a good thing." He forces a smile, letting me know he's not being honest. Maybe he's lying to both of us. I hate that for him. "Anyway, let me set the pizza inside and then we'll go get you a Christmas tree before it gets too dark."

"Aren't we eating first?"

"Not if we don't want to be chopping down trees in the dark."

"I guess you're right."

He smirks. "That's something that happens a lot around me."

Giggling, I watch him walk towards the house, admiring his backside. The moment he steps through the door, I move, taking my time climbing out of the truck as I wait for him. He returns, pulling an ax out of the back of his truck. A mischievous glint shines in his eyes as he stares at me, his voice monotone. "Let's go."

I laugh, stepping towards him. "Don't you want a coat?"

His crooked smile slips out. "Nah, I have plenty to keep me warm."

Surprising me, he reaches down, grabbing my hand, entwining our fingers together. My heart pounds erratically and I attempt to focus on the trees while I get my heart under control. "So, where are the best trees under eight feet?"

"This way," he directs with a gentle tug.

We walk hand in hand down the dirt path, covered in fallen leaves, the scent of pine thick in the air. I smile to myself, the moment surreal. I've had a crush on this man for a long time, but I've also repeatedly been warned. I've heard the stories, but he's been so caring, protective, perfect…maybe the warnings are unjust.

His phone rings, breaking the silence. He pulls it out glancing at the screen before quickly tapping ignore and slipping it back in his pocket. Unfortunately, he wasn't fast enough. "Who's Lace?"

If I weren't staring at him, I might not notice his flinch, but I do. "No one important."

Then again, maybe the warnings are spot on. "What about this one?" I point to a tree, about a foot taller than Dean.

"This one? You sure?"

I nod and he drops my hand, stepping up to the tree I've claimed as mine, for no other reason than it's a decent tree and my head tells me not to believe in happily ever after no matter what my heart wants. What am I doing, especially after that phone call? Does he want to be here with me? I hold my breath as I watch him take out his frustrations in a few swings. The tree falls, landing with an echoing thump. Grabbing the tree in one hand, the ax in the other, he turns back towards his house with me trailing behind.

The silence is no longer peaceful between us. I quicken my pace just to keep up and I hate it.

57

Chapter 12

Dean

The moment the text from Lace, a late-night hookup, came through, the air shifted. Leah looked physically pained and quickly tried to hide it, but it was too late. She's too damn good for me. I wasn't kidding when I said Lace was no one important. She uses me for my body. For me, that's something I feel like I have at least some control over. This thing with Leah, whatever it is, has me losing all common sense.

We walk into my place, the living, dining, and kitchen area in an L-shape with the chocolate brown leather couch and recliner in front of the TV to my right, a round table behind it to my left, with the kitchen in the back on the left. I make my way into the kitchen, turning on the oven and sliding the pizza in to warm it up before daring a glance at Leah. She tugs her white coat in as if she's cold, protecting herself from me.

Heaving a sigh, I step closer, planting my hands on the counter as I watch her looking around my place, avoiding my gaze. "Maybe I should just take you home." The words are out before I think it through.

"What? Do you want me to go?"

The look on her face makes me wince and I shake my head, giving her the truth. "No, but you don't look like you want to be here anymore."

"I'm sorry."

"Stop, there's nothing for you to apologize for."

She offers me a sad smile, squeezing my heart. "Why me?" My eyes widen in shock. "I mean, you could have anyone you want and with me, things could get sticky. So why me? Is it because of what happened the other night?"

I scoff, my disbelief apparent. "I think the better question would be why I should stay away from you. You're way too good for me, Lee."

"That's not true." She rolls her eyes dramatically, reminding me of when I first met her. I was at her house and she walked through the door, looking young, but fierce, angry about a mean girl at school. She still has the same fire in her eyes. I never want to be the one to take that away from her; it's one of the things that makes her so special. "And Lee?" she quirks a brow.

I shrug. "A different nickname for the sexy grownup Leah." Stepping around the counter, I move in front of her, tucking a loose blonde lock of hair behind her ear. She looks up at me with wide eyes, her breathing picking up its pace and her eyes deepening to a darker blue making my body stand up and take notice. "And it is true. You're beautiful, smart, and determined. You work your ass off to get what you want; you would never expect someone to just hand it to you. You make me laugh without even trying and your heart is pure gold.”

“Dean,” she whispers my name, the sound hitting like an electric shock, going both to my chest and my dick.

My body moves without thinking. Cradling her face in my hands, I lower my mouth to hers. Moving my lips slow and fluid, I relish the warmth, the sweet taste, the spark as she kisses me back, moaning softly into my mouth. Her tongue juts out, licking my lips and I’m done for.

I pull back barely breathing. “You’re too good for me, Leah, but damn I want you,” I growl over her lips, holding her heated gaze. Without delay, I mold my mouth to hers, my tongue slipping into her mouth, finding hers in an eager dance. With our teeth clashing, tongues licking, and mouths sucking, I pull her to me, lifting her up, and setting her on the counter for better access. I step between her legs and she tugs frantically at my hair, her tongue matching mine, tasting like mint and vanilla; spicy and sweet like her.

The oven beeps, piercing our bubble. Startled, I break our kiss, breathing heavy. I stare at her, her chest rapidly rising and falling, her cheeks flushed, and her hair no longer perfect. When did she get so fucking gorgeous?

As I try to catch my breath, I step over her discarded coat and pull the pizza out of the oven. Why is her coat on the floor and when did she take it off? Or was that me? I run my hand through my hair, exhaling harshly. I need to slow the fuck down.

"Hungry?"

Chapter 13

Leah

What the hell just happened? And can we do that again? I've never been kissed like that, with so much passion, desperation. His kiss breathed life into me and I don't want to live without it after diving into the waters. Does he kiss all women like that? Women like Lace?

"What's wrong?" Dean asks, his eyebrows drawn down in concern. I remain silent, looking at him with confusion. I've never wanted anything more. At the same time, I refuse to be just another notch on his bedpost. "Your face is scrunched up like you're upset."

Lace. Her name won't leave the forefront of my mind. I nod and lie through my teeth, "No, I was just thinking about something for the event."

"Do you need help with anything?"

I laugh, my body relaxing as we sit at the counter, eating pizza and talking about work. It feels normal. It's just what I need. "Yeah, there's still a ton to do. I just hope it goes smoothly. Working with twenty-five different organizations is a lot. We have one person from our company overseeing two or three each and I'm coordinating the kickoff event, along with the *25 Men of Christmas* calendar we're giving out Thursday. You'll also be able to buy a digital copy, but it will only be available for the month of December."

"What did you do with the other six days of December?"

"Like I said, we had some earlier promo shots done, some group shots and those filled in the last few days perfectly."

"I can't believe you're getting it done so fast."

"It took a lot of persistence and begging."

"Well, I'm impressed. I've been working for my family business for a long time and it takes weeks for me to get any quality printing done.

I pause, pursing my lips, staring at him in thought. "What is it you do exactly? Joe never told me what your family business is or what you do for a living."

He grins. "One of the reasons I know I can trust him."

I startle, taken aback. "You know you can trust him because he didn't tell his sister what you do?"

He chuckles softly and shrugs. "Yeah." I narrow my eyes, but he only laughs harder. "I told you before, people are assholes when money is involved."

"But I'm not them."

He gets a look in his eyes that makes it difficult to breathe as he stares at me, his gaze holding me captive. With a shake of his head, he breaks our moment. "No, you're not." Keeping his eyes fixed on me, he continues, "My family owns a lot of land and they've invested in different businesses over the years. One of those businesses is private jets."

"Jets?"

His stare grows more intense as he elaborates. "That's what I do. I use my business degree to run Chambers Luxury Fleet. It's a private jet sales and rental company."

"Hm," I mumble, more curious than anything. "Can you fly them?"

"I have my pilot license."

"Wow, okay." I nod as he continues watching me closely making me feel like my under a microscope, but I'm not sure why. "Do you like what you do?"

He pauses, licking his lips and drawing my attention. My gaze snaps back to his eyes as he clears his throat. "Yeah, I do. I like the freedom it gives me. I enjoy flying and traveling. And I think I'm damn good at the business side of things. We work with mostly corporate or rich assholes; sometimes both." He smirks. "But I handle it and do it well."

"I'm not surprised." His features soften. "But didn't you go to University of Southern Maine?"

He huffs a laugh. "You know I did."

"Why?" He quirks a brow. "It's a great school, I'm just surprised you didn't end up somewhere more…elite."

He grimaces. "It's not me. My parents wanted me somewhere else, but in the end, they didn't care enough to fight me on it. I wanted to be somewhere I could blend in, somewhere people didn't know who I was, or who my family was, and like you said, it's a great school. But it also gave me a chance to enjoy college without the pressure of my family name."

"Well, from the stories I've heard, you took full advantage of that." The words slip out before I can stop them and I swiftly snap my mouth shut, my eyes wide.

He flinches, quickly hiding it. "Yeah."

Clearing my throat, I try to bring him back to me, asking another question. "No one ever knew?"

He shrugs. "People found out, but I could usually tell by the way they treated me. I got sick of being used in one way or another. Joe and Christian were the only two that never asked for anything from me except my friendship. We always have each other's backs. I will never do anything to put that in jeopardy."

My head rears back, his words feeling like a slap to the face. It's not like I would ever tell my brother we kissed, but I guess that means we can never be anything more and I'm already in too deep. I've had this stupid crush on him for years. I need to get over it. It's time to change the subject. "That explains why you were able to help me out at the last minute."

"I'm happy to play Santa to help you with anything you desire." A crooked grin covers his face making my heart skip a beat and my skin heat. Attempting to ignore him, I take a bite of my pizza, but this sexy man and his playful innuendos are not easy to overlook. What am I going to do?

Chapter 14

Dean

"Ding!"

The elevator doors slide open but I hesitate, wondering if I should be here. Leah might not appreciate me just showing up, but from everything she told me, she'll work right through lunch to make sure everything is perfect and she needs to eat. I can't help but question why I feel the need to be the one to take care of her.

Someone bumps into me as they step past me, jolting me out of my thoughts. "Sorry," the guy mumbles. "Hey, you're one of our models, aren't you?"

I lift my head, glancing at a tall, thin guy with brown hair and eyes. "I guess I am."

He laughs. "Not your normal thing? So, what are you in for today?"

"Just checking in with a *friend*." I grimace, the word feeling wrong on my tongue.

"Need help, finding your *friend*? They won't let you by the front desk without an appointment."

A heavy sigh escapes my lips, his words making me second-guess myself again. But I'm here, so I don't hesitate. "Leah Abrams."

He grins, nodding his head. "Leah," he murmurs, dragging out her name, succeeding in pissing me off. I bite my tongue, waiting for the doors to open. "Follow me."

I glare at his back as we walk down the hall and into a large conference room. Leah stands at the front, intently studying pictures spread out in front of her and some jackass looming behind her. "Leah, you have a *friend* here to see you," the guy announces, further irritating me.

She lifts her head, pushing her blonde hair behind her ear. Her gaze crashes with mine, a smile immediately tugging at her lips. "Dean, what are you doing here?"

I approach, feigning my usual confidence. "Hey, I thought you might be hungry and with the event Thursday night, I was fairly confident you would skip lunch if I didn't force it on you."

She laughs, the sound going straight through me. "You're right." She steps away from the tables and towards me, forcing the dickhead to move back. "Thank you." She smiles up at me, the look making my dick twitch.

I clear my throat. "So, are you going to eat, or do I need to force-feed you?"

"Well, your timing is perfect. I guess I can take a few minutes with you." She smirks, turning back towards the dickhead. "You can take lunch and we can finish up this afternoon."

"Okay. See you in a bit," he calls, her focus already on me and I fucking love it.

She looks gorgeous in black pants, a matching blazer, and a red silk tank underneath, with her hair pulled up into a messy bun, a pen sticking through it. I point to it, arching my eyebrows in question. A blush covers her cheeks as she grabs the pen and tugs, her blonde hair spilling over her shoulders. "I just needed my hair out of the way. We were looking through pictures we want included with the decorations and my hair kept falling in my face. It's easier, and…" She shakes her head, her nerves going along with it. "What's for lunch?"

The combination of her nerves and her confidence is like my favorite candy on Christmas morning, making me want to do something stupid like lay her out on the conference table and claim her as mine. Shoving the thought away, I focus on lunch. "I wasn't sure what you would want, but I got a chicken salad sandwich with cranberries and a turkey club with cranberry dressing."

Arching her eyebrows she asks, "What if I don't like cranberry?"

"It's Christmas-y. You don't have a choice."

She laughs. "Well, it's a good thing I love it, then."

"Yeah, it's a good thing your brother is my best friend."

Her lips twitch as she gives me a look attempting to keep a straight face, but a giggle escapes as she steps past me. "Come on, we can sit down here."

She reaches for the chicken salad and I hand her a water, sitting down next to her. "I hope it's okay I just showed up."

"It's sweet. Thank you."

I nod. "When do you actually start decorating for Thursday?"

"Luckily, we get into the venue to start setting up on Wednesday morning. There's no way we would get it done in one day."

"Are we still decorating your tree tonight?"

Frowning, she groans. "If I ever get out of here. I keep telling myself, a few more days and then someone else takes over."

"You need to make it to Thursday night. Let me help you."

"You've already done so much."

"Not enough if you're still stressed," I claim, my hand falling to her knee, tingles shooting up my arm. She turns to me, her blue eyes darkening like the sea, pulling me in. Without thought, I lean towards her, caressing her cheek and pressing my lips to hers. Her hand falls to my arm as she kisses me back, my heart squeezing.

"Would you look at that…" his deep voice grumbles as he steps into the room. Leah pulls back and jumps up, as the world crashes around us. I move with her, her body trembling. "All I had to do is pretend to be a hero and it would be Merry Fucking Christmas to me.”

I lunge, but her arms wrap around my waist, urging me to stop. “Don’t,” she pleads so quietly I almost don’t hear.

“What the fuck are you doing here?” I challenge, stepping in front of Leah, attempting to block her from view. He has no right to ever look at her again.

“I was invited. I have an event to attend on Thursday and I have a meeting with my new contact.”

Leah gasps, pressing further into my back. “You’re not going to the event,” I command like I have every right.

He laughs. “But I did nothing wrong in the eyes of the law. You, on the other hand…”

Before I have a chance to realize what’s happening, Leah is in front of me, stepping towards him. “You stay the hell away from him and me or I will make your life a living hell,” she threatens with conviction that makes me cower.

“Damn, I bet you’re a firecracker in bed.”

Surprising me, she lunges for him with an animalistic growl. My hand wraps around her waist, lifting until her feet leave the floor. “Let me go.”

“I think he’s the one who needs to go,” I argue, my blood boiling, but reigning in my temper to take care of the woman in my arms.

He laughs, waving as he walks out the door. "I'll see you both later."

My hold loosens as he waltzes out the door like he owns the fucking place. Pushing away from me, Leah collapses into the seat she just vacated. Fuck.

Chapter 15

Leah

Why would they let him come into the office? After what happened, I don't understand. My boss's words echo in my head. "He's gone, Leah and this time he won't be back."

I groan, running my hands through my hair. I hate that he'll still be in the calendar, but there's not enough time to replace him, although I'm not going to stop looking. Thankfully he's banned from the event and the office.

A knock at the door startles me out of my thoughts. "Coming!"

I yank the door open, my heart skipping a beat at the sight of Dean standing in my doorway with a crooked grin. "What are you doing here?"

"Are you at least a little happy to see me? I brought hot chocolate." He waves two cups in front of me.

"Of course, come in." He steps past me, handing me a cup. I close the door and take a sip, moaning in appreciation, "Mm."

"You're trying to kill me, aren't you?"

My eyes fly open, instantly spotting the heat in his eyes. I grin. "For the record, I would've let you in without the hot chocolate, but this gives you bonus points."

"I'll take it." We make our way to the couch and sit down, the boxes of decorations still unopened in front of the tree. "Is your roommate home?"

"No, she's out with friends."

He nods, his voice soft, asking, "You okay?"

I meet his gaze and sigh. "Yeah. I think I'm more mad than anything with how it was handled."

"I agree with that." His jaw clenches and he gives a slight shake of his head. "So, I have the rest of the week off, and I thought I could help you out with the event."

"What? Do you ever work?"

He chuckles and shrugs his shoulders. "Of course, but I am my own boss and you are my priority."

"Dean, I can protect myself."

"I know. You've proven that, but I won't get anything done after today. This is for me."

I scoff, knowing that's only half the truth, but I don't care. "Fine, but I have to clear it with my boss."

He winces. "I already did. I introduced myself and asked if I could help."

"Introduced yourself?" The look in his eyes tells me his statement means more than he's claiming.

Shifting uncomfortably, he runs his hand through his hair. "Yeah, my name and company."

My heart sinks, knowing he gave up his anonymity for me. "I'm sorry."

"Don't," he warns, his jaw clenching as he stares at me, pleading. I snap my mouth shut. My stomach twists, and I gulp down the sudden lump in my throat as realization slams into me. He really cares about me, but what does that mean for him?

Stop, Leah. Don't get your hopes up. I'm not ready to go there. Pushing my questions away, I nod, my gaze veering towards the tree. "Well, you brought the hot chocolate. How about we turn on some Christmas music and you can help me decorate my tree?"

He grins, the tension easing out of him. "I like that plan."

I flip on the satellite holiday radio station and connect it to my speaker, a new version of *All I Want for Christmas* blasting throughout the room. Dean wiggles his eyebrows playfully, making me laugh as we open up the boxes, finding the ornaments. "Are these all yours?"

"Mostly. Scarlett has a few, but she has all her decorations in the box against the wall."

I pull out a reindeer ornament, and he grabs a Santa, bringing it close to his face. "See the resemblance?"

Another giggle escapes and his mouth drops open, feigning offense. I only laugh harder and he's soon joining in. "I like playful Dean."

He steps closer, reaching over me to hang Santa on the other side of the tree. As he brings his hand back, his fingers graze the side of my face. "I like laughing Leah." Did he just say he likes me? My heart races, but he steps back without leaning in, smiling down at me.

Trying to shake it off, I grab a roller skate, reminding me of a Christmas when I was small. "One Christmas, I begged for roller skates. I asked Santa for ones with pom-poms and told my parents my life would be over if I didn't get them." He laughs. "I know, but I could be a bit dramatic when I wanted. Anyway, I got the roller skates and I was so excited, I had to try them right away, but since it was freezing outside my parents told me I had to wait, so I had to be creative." I shrug, smirking. "How could they honestly expect me to wait to use the present I'd been begging for?"

He laughs again, the sound giving me goosebumps. "So, I snuck down into the basement and tried them on, trying to skate around on the cement, but we didn't have the space for it."

"Oh, no."

I nod. "Yeah. I lost my balance, my arms flailing like a windmill and fell hard, breaking my arm and slicing my elbow open. I was afraid I'd get into trouble, so I hid down there crying until Joe found me and convinced me to come upstairs by telling me he ate all the candy from my stocking."

Dean's head falls back, laughing. "Joe?"

"I know, right?" I grin. "Anyway, it worked. And while I was trying to look in my stocking, my dad found me covered in blood like something out of a horror movie and brought me to the hospital. I never wanted to roller skate again.

The next Christmas, Joe got me this telling me that it's the only skate I should ever have. Of course, after that I had to prove him wrong and saved up my money to buy a new pair of skates since my old ones were too small at that point. Then, I finally learned how to skate. That's one of my favorite Christmas memories; obviously not getting hurt, but realizing how strong I am."

"Determination is beautiful on you, Leah."

My stomach flips. "Thank you. I'll always find a way to stand up and push forward. I won't let anyone or anything keep me down."

He steps towards me, the intensity shining in his eyes overwhelming. "Damn," he mumbles, running his hands over my hair, grasping my neck, and tipping my head back. He runs his thumb over my lower lip. My breath catches as he tips his head down, kissing me soft and slow, as if he has all the time in the world igniting me from the inside-out. I moan, pushing up on my tiptoes, attempting to get closer, but he pulls back. Dizzy from his kiss, I drop back on my heels, slightly stunned.

That kiss felt nothing like the player I've been warned about.

Chapter 16

Dean

The next day, I stayed at the office with Leah as she worked into the night. There was no way in hell I was going to leave her side. I would find every excuse I could to help. She'll be fine. Her strength is attractive as fuck, but I needed to see this through for my own peace of mind.

Hopefully she won't kill me for what I did with her *25 Men of Christmas* countdown calendar. Sometimes it's good to be known; this was one of those times.

Working alongside some of her staff, we unload the decorations followed by a truck of calendars, placing them on a table at the front of the event venue. "December 5th, you're looking fine!" Scarlett smirks.

I shake my head in amusement. "Gee, thanks."

She continues flipping through the calendar and suddenly gasps. Her gaze wavers between me and the calendar. "You did this, didn't you?"

"Yup," I murmur, popping the p.

"Did she see this yet?"

"Nope."

"Damn…" She spins on her heel and yells across the room. "Hey, Leah, your calendars are here. You should see these."

Eyes wide with panic, she stops what she's doing and rushes over. "Are they okay? Please tell me they're okay."

Scarlett holds her hand up. "Whoa. Nothing to worry about. I promise."

Leah eyes her friend as she picks up the calendar and begins flipping through. Her eyes flare, pausing a little longer on December 5th, causing my lips to curve up. I can't help it. She continues skimming through, until she reaches December 21st and screams, the calendar flying out of her hands onto the floor. "What is that?"

"That," Scarlett points to the discarded calendar, "is Saint Nick making sure the devil didn't end up in your Christmas calendar."

"What?" Slowly, she turns to me with wide, teary eyes, my heart clenching. "Dean?"

I blush, nodding, not sure if she's happy, pissed or a little of both. In the next instant she crashes into me, squeezing me tight. My arms fall to her back as my cheek rests on top of her head, my pent-up breath leaving me. "Thank you," she rasps, her breath catching.

"Anything for you," I whisper, unsure if she hears me.

She pushes back, stepping out of my embrace and wiping away her tears. "But did it have to be my brother?"

My head falls back as I burst out laughing. There's my girl. The simple thought causes my heart to thunder in my chest as my laughter slows, reality slamming into me. I'm falling for Leah. Fuck. Clearing my throat, I clarify, "So you're not pissed I messed with your calendar?"

She grins. "Nah, just that it's my brother." She scrunches her nose up. "But how in the world did you get Joe to agree?"

I smirk. "I have my ways."

She shakes her head, giggling, the light sound going right through me. "In other words, I don't want to know." I shrug, unapologetic. I would do it again in a heartbeat to protect her. And besides, the asshole didn't deserve a single bit of the attention he'd likely garner from something like this. It would only fuel the flames. I'm sure that's the last thing any of these companies would want. "Why don't you come help me with the auction room?"

"Lead the way."

We cover the tables, alternating red and green tablecloths before spreading out the various auction items. She gasps. "You donated a private jet?"

I chuckle. "Not exactly. I donated a private jet for a one-week getaway in California wine country. I couldn't exactly donate one without the other."

Her smile lights up her face. "Thank you!"

I nod, not wanting the praise. She reads me right, changing the subject. "So, we talked about one of my favorite Christmas memories the other day, but you never told me yours."

"You're right." I continue working, not wanting to meet her gaze as I confess. "Honestly, my favorite memory is watching you, Joe, and the rest of your family the year Joe brought me for Christmas Eve. It was our junior year of college. Christian was home with Bree and his family. Joe knew my parents were gone." I smile at the memory. "I've never had a Christmas like that, where it's really about family. Your house had the kind of love and laughter, that I barely caught glimpses of growing up."

Leah's hand falls to my arm, her voice soft, squeezing my heart. "Dean?"

I shake my head and force a smile. "It's okay, I can't complain. I haven't had a bad life at all. They just didn't believe much in holidays."

"That sucks."

I laugh. "Yeah, it does, but I turned out just fine."

She scrunches her nose up adorably. "Well…" she murmurs, dragging out the word.

"Hey!" I reach for her and she giggles as I squeeze her side.

She settles as my arms inch around her, like that's exactly where she's meant to be, the feeling itself foreign to me. "Dean?"

"Hmm?"

"What about this Christmas? Do you have plans?"

"Right now, I'm focused on you." My lips find hers, as my hands weave into her hair. My tongue slips out, licking her lips. Her mouth opens, allowing me entry. Our tongues meet in the middle, giving me a sweet taste before she falls back on her heels, breathless.

She licks her lips, her gaze hungry. "Come home with me tonight."

I groan, my dick standing at attention and ready to follow, but this is Leah. I can't dive in before knowing that I'm really what she wants. "Fuck, I want to, Leah. But I need you to be sure. Joe is my best friend and I can't fuck that up. I can't do that to him and I sure as hell can't do that to you."

Her face falls and she nods, looking rejected. "Okay."

"Leah." I palm her face in my hand, needing her to look at me. "I want you."

"I know."

"What about this… Take the day to think about what you want. We have the event tomorrow and I plan on keeping you in bed after this is over if you still want this." I pause, gesturing between the two of us. "You and me."

She looks up at me, thoughtful. "I can do that, Dean, but I'm not about to change my mind."

A salacious grin tugs at my lips. "I sure as fuck hope that's true."

She pushes up on her tiptoes, giving me one more chaste kiss and walks away, my dick throwing insults my way.

Chapter 17

Leah

I'm so nervous, but not for tonight's event. At this point, I know I've done all I can. I'm sure there will be a few last-minute fires anyone can handle, but I expect it to go well. It's Dean that's making my stomach go haywire and my body twitch in anticipation of what's to come and hoping he doesn't change his mind.

I can't stop running my fingers over the red silky fabric of my A-line dress. The top has spaghetti straps with a V-neck accented with a fitted, lace floral overlay, while the bottom fans out just enough so I'm able to move around freely. Although I've opted for a two-inch heel, wanting to be closer to Dean's lips, hopefully my heels won't be my downfall.

Ugh, I sound ridiculous, even in my own head. I've crushed on him for so long, and now that he wants me, how do I jump in and still protect my heart? Doesn't he get it? But there's no way I'm changing my mind. It's Dean.

I wonder what Joe would say if he found out. My stomach drops, but I quickly shake the thought away and shove my brother out of my mind. He's the last thing I want to think about right now.

Scarlett walks into the bathroom, her eyes meeting mine in the mirror as she smiles. "Everything looks fantastic out there! You did such a great job."

I grin, spinning around. "Thank you. You look gorgeous, Scar."

She curtsies in her shimmering dark green mermaid dress, her red locks hanging loose around her shoulders. "Thanks. So do you, Leah. Dean is going to have a coronary when he sees you."

I blush, brushing away her comment. "Are the models done with the prep?"

She smirks. "What you really want to know is Dean done? Yes, but not everyone is yet. I'm sure they'll all be ready when the doors open."

I nod, taking a deep breath and exhaling slowly. "Well, then, a little more lipstick and let's go." She laughs and we both reapply before slipping out the bathroom door. Bypassing the white lights, the Christmas trees, the wreaths, the garland, and the rest of the Christmas decorations, my eyes drift towards the Safe Haven Alliance, where I know Dean will be standing in support. He's wearing a classic black tuxedo with a red vest and bow tie taking my breath away.

"Is there anything he doesn't look good in?" Scarlett asks.

My stomach twists as I take him in. "No," I answer honestly, just as he turns and meets my gaze, his eyes blazing from across the room. "I should go say hi to him before he gets busy."

"Yeah, you do that." She giggles and turns in the other direction.

My heart thrashes against my ribcage as I approach, Dean's eyes never leaving mine, holding me captive. "Wow," he mutters under his breath. "Leah, you're absolutely breathtaking."

My skin heats as I smile adoringly up at him. "Thank you, Dean. You look pretty good yourself."

"Thanks." He grins, leaning down, placing a kiss on the corner of my lips. Goosebumps instantly erupt across my skin, my eyes darting around us before returning to him. "This looks incredible, Lee. You've done a really good thing."

"Thank you. I just want it to go well."

"It will."

Joe steps up between us with a wide grin. "Leah, this is, wow."

I turn to my brother, smiling. "Thanks for coming."

He smirks and gestures to Dean. "Well, you know I wanted to come, but honestly, this guy twisted my arm. I couldn't say no."

"Well, thank you both. I should go check on everyone else." They both wave as I spin on my heel and walk away, ready for the night to be over before it even begins.

Soon the night is in full swing, the rooms packed with supporters of the various organizations and the local news. The *25 Men of Christmas countdown* calendars, alongside the men themselves, are the night's biggest success. I should be happy, but my gaze keeps drifting to Dean, finding him taking pictures with women and sometimes men hanging off him, laughing, talking, and having a good time. I shouldn't be surprised, he's not only sexy as hell, but he's doing exactly what's been asked of him. Unfortunately, the jealous pull I have in my gut doesn't give a damn and wants to claim him in front of everyone. Well, everyone except Joe.

I attempt to push the thought away when a memory of one of Joe's warnings flashes in my mind. *Dean always could talk a woman into doing almost anything he wanted.* My stomach churns, but I remind myself, I'm the one who started this. If anyone is trying to do the convincing, it's me. I know what I want. Does he?

Sighing, I push my dark thoughts away and make my way around the room, posing with each organization and model, documenting the event. As I move to step away from Joe, he wraps me in a hug and whispers in my ear, "I'm so damn proud to be your brother."

"I love you," I rasp, too choked up to say more before I make my escape.

By the time I circle back around to Dean, the night is almost over. He gives me his crooked smile causing my heart to race, pounding against my ribcage. His arm falls around me, pulling me close as we pose for another picture. "You're a busy woman tonight, everyone wants a piece of you."

"I was just thinking the same about you."

He arches his eyebrows, waving away my comment. Taking a deep breath, I gather my courage and catch his gaze, making sure he knows my intentions. "The night is almost over. Dean, I need you to know, I haven't changed my mind. I know what I want." His eyes flare as he stares down at me. "Do you?"

Holding my gaze, he gulps hard and gives me a firm nod. "I have absolutely no doubt in my mind about what and who I want. Tell me when you can go because I'm not leaving here without you."

I give him a firm nod, his hand falling away from my back as I turn and walk away. My stomach tightens as I wait, not able to think about anything else but him. Glancing at the time, my muscles tense, the end of the night dragging, the seconds ticking by. My thoughts remain on nothing but one man; Dean.

Chapter 18

Dean

My hands press against her doorframe vibrating with need as I wait for her to unlock her door. "Is your roommate home?"

"I think so…"

The key clicks and we push inside. Spinning her around, I pick her up as I kick the door closed behind me. "Wrap your legs around me." She does as I say, tossing her coat on the floor as she kisses and licks a path down my neck, searing my skin.

"First door on the left."

I shove inside her room, turning her around, pinning her against her door, devouring her mouth. My tongue slips inside, tasting, licking, exploring, desperate for her. Pushing her dress up, I press my body to hers, groaning as my cock rubs against her heat, feeling like I could burst before we begin.

Her head falls back against the door as my hands begin to roam, my body holding her in place, not bothering to remove her sexy as sin dress. My hands skim over her breasts, her belly, her ass, not sure what I want to explore first. "Dean," she whimpers, my name a desperate plea as she tugs on my hair. The sound goes straight to my balls.

"Fuck, Lee, I need you."

"Please. I can't wait anymore." She shoves my tux jacket off my shoulders and I pause, reaching into the inside pocket, and grabbing a condom before I shake the jacket to the floor. She reaches down and rubs me through my pants, making me groan. "Please."

I reach down, sliding her panties to the side and finding her soaked. "Fuck, yes." I drop my pants and boxers, rolling on the condom, still holding her in place. With a quick yank on the sides of her panties, I drop them to the floor and line up, looking into her eyes for consent.

She arches towards me, pressing her lips to mine, giving me what I need. I plunge inside, not able to take it slow, not yet. A guttural groan leaves our lips. Grasping her knees, I push them towards her chest and thrust, determined to make her feel as good as she's making me. My balls, slap against her heat as my dick dives deep inside her, my vision starting to blur.

"Dean," she screams, tugging my hair, my shirt, anything she can grab. I move faster, harder, deeper, eager to see her come undone in my arms.

My balls start to tingle, letting me know I'm close. "Lee, I can't…hold…on…please." White flashes, body burning, and my balls explode. My movements become erratic as her insides squeeze my cock. We groan, pushing, thrusting, desperate, until she collapses against me, both of us panting for breath.

Holy fuck that was hot.

I take a minute to get my bearings before I release her knees, kissing her softly before letting her slide down my body, her dress falling into place. She looks up at me, slightly timid, making my lips twitch. Leaning down, I weave my fingers into her hair and kiss her again, deeper, trying to let her know I'm not going anywhere. "You okay?"

She nods awkwardly, making me chuckle. "Yeah, just, wow…"

I grin, kicking my shoes off and stepping out of my pants before removing the condom, and tossing it in the garbage by her desk. "We need to get you out of that dress."

"But we just…"

I nod, not able to wipe the smile off my face. "Yeah, but now I need to take my time and cherish every bit of you I didn't get the chance to explore."

She whimpers, the sound vibrating through me. "Okay."

My fingers trail down her shoulders, between her breasts, her skin velvety soft. "I didn't even see you yet. There's so much to do."

"Dean," she moans. She turns around, moving her hair to the side.

My hands slide to her waist, undoing her dress. Tracing a trail up her spine, I slip her straps off her shoulders, letting it pool around her feet, her heels her only accessory. When she doesn't move, my arm wraps around her waist and I pick her up, tossing her lightly onto her bed. She giggles and rolls over, looking up at me.

I stop, taking in her beauty, with her blonde hair splayed above her head. Her flawless ivory skin, her full breasts and taut pink nipples, the curve of her waist and a thin strip leading down to her sweet pussy. The sight of her brings my dick back to life. "You're so beautiful."

She blushes that shade of red I love so much. "What about you? I think you need to get rid of the rest of your clothes."

I glance down, my shirt, vest, and tie still in place, a couple buttons ripped off making me chuckle. With her eyes on me, I peel them off and crawl over her as if she's my prey. She reaches up and pulls me to her lips, her tongue slipping inside. Moaning I pull back, leaning on my left arm and kissing my way to her breast, while my other hand skates across her skin. My tongue sticks out, swirling around her nipple and sucking it into my mouth, my hand, rolling and pinching her other one, craving her soft sounds as she arches into me. Releasing, I switch sides, giving each the same treatment.

I move down her body, my fingers finding her wet folds, I groan, slipping inside, her answering moan making me harder. My mouth finds her clit, as I add a finger, curling them inside. My tongue juts out, licking, savoring her sweet taste. "Dean! Ah!" Circling her clit with my tongue, I move in slow, deliberate strokes, relishing every sound, every taste, every reaction. She bucks underneath me. I lay my palm on her stomach, pinning her to the mattress as I work her body. She screams, just before her insides squeeze my fingers and her juices explode on my tongue, continuing my assault until her body gives in, melting into the mattress.

She laughs. "What are you doing to me?"

My lips tug upwards. "What we both want."

Reaching for me, her hand slides up and down my shaft. "How are you hard again?"

"You." She starts to slide down my body, but I stop her with a shake of my head. "One more orgasm from you with me inside you."

She jumps out of bed, reaching into my tuxedo pocket, and finding five more condoms. Arching her eyebrows, she questions, "Confident?"

"Hopeful." I shrug, nonapologetic.

She comes back with one, tearing it open, and rolling it on before straddling me and easing herself onto my cock. My head falls back as I watch her move. Groaning, I flip her over, taking control. I press my lips to hers, our tongues fighting for dominance as we move in a slow, sensual rhythm. My hands drift to her breasts, rolling her nipples between my fingers, increasing our pace. As my balls begin to tighten, my hand slides lower, circling her clit. Breaking our kiss, I plead, "I need you to cum."

Our breathing becomes rapid, matching our thrusts, the sound of skin slapping against skin echoing in the room. "Dean."

Her body convulses around mine, squeezing me, milking me urging my body into bliss.

My vision blurs, my body goes taut, burning like a raging inferno as I fall over the edge once again, bright light dancing behind my eyelids. Groaning, I pump into her a few more times as my body comes down from a high like I've never known. Breathing heavily, I collapse next to her.

Taking a moment, I catch my breath before disposing of the condom. Rushing back to Leah, I pull her into my arms, her head resting on my chest. I kiss the top of her head, whispering, "I didn't know it could be like this." She doesn't respond, but I don't care. For the first time I believe we have all the time in the world.

Chapter 19

Leah

My eyes flutter open, my body wrapped around Dean causing a smile to tug at my lips and my body to heat.

"Good morning, Lee," his deep voice rumbles my skin as he runs his hands through my hair.

"Morning." I lift my head, looking up at him. The sight of his heated gaze making my heart pound.

He pulls me to him, pressing his lips to mine. His mouth moves over mine in a sweet rhythm, his kiss soft and slow as he cradles my face in his hands. "Mm," I moan, my body burning and my core wet instantly.

"Ready for another round?" He flips me over, his lips falling to my neck, my back arching, curving into his body, as he wakes me up in every way. A knock at the door, causes a soft growl of protest to escape his lips.

Another knock, a little bit louder interrupts his movements, my brother's voice silencing further protests. "Leah, are you in there? I need to talk to you about Christmas and you're not answering your phone."

My eyes widen in panic. Joe can't see Dean here. "Give me a minute!" I yell as I scramble out of bed and throw on my clothes. I glance at Dean, staring at me, unmoving. "What are you doing? You have to get out of bed. You have to hide."

His eyes widen. "What?"

Glancing towards the closed front door and back at Dean, my panic surges. "You have to hide. Joe can't see you here."

His mouth falls slightly open, looking like he's about to argue, but he presses his lips together and throws the covers off making my mouth water. I shake my head to get my head straight while he does as I request, trudging into the bathroom. "I'm too old for this shit," he grumbles under his breath, making me wince.

"I'm sorry," I whisper, as the door closes softly behind him.

Sighing, I rush towards the front door and yank it open, my brother leaning against the doorframe. "Took you long enough," he grumbles pushing off and stepping inside.

"Sorry, I was up late with the event and it's been a long couple months. I needed the sleep."

"I'm sure you did. It looked like everything went great. The place was packed. Did you get a good read on how it went?"

I smile. "It went really well. I think all the organizations are thrilled with the results so far. There's still more time."

"That's great, Leah. I'm proud of you."

My brother wraps his arms around me, giving me a hug, and bring a smile to my face. "Thanks, Joe."

He releases me, taking a step back. "You're welcome. By the way, how did it work out with Dean?"

"He was fantastic! Thank you so much for sending him." I rave.

"No problem. You two sure seemed pretty cozy just before the event began." Joe's eyes narrow.

"Yeah, I've gotten to know him better since I've been working with him. He's a good guy." Joe crosses his arms over his chest, watching me close. My heart races and with a shake of my head, I begin rambling trying to wipe that look off my brother's face. "But, you know Dean, he seemed to relish every moment with so many women and even a few men draped over him all night. I'm sure he's happy with all the phone numbers I'm sure he collected from doing the calendar."

He laughs humorlessly, his hand running along his jaw. "Sure…"

My stomach churns, my entire body on edge. "I'm sorry to kick you out, but I have to get ready to go meet up with Scarlett to go Christmas shopping. She stopped at her parents, but I overslept and I don't want her waiting too long."

"Okay, I just need to talk to you about Christmas."

"I know, but not right now. I've just been busy, but with the event over, my big part is done and it's someone else's responsibility now. I promise, I'll respond next time you text or call. We can figure out Christmas later, okay? I really have to go," I insist, my teeth running nervously over my lower lip.

"Okay, okay." He laughs, putting his hands up in surrender. "I can take a hint. I'll catch up with you later. Great job, Leah."

"Thanks," I mumble, walking him towards the door, desperate to get him out of here. "Bye, Joe." He waves as I close the door behind him.

Heaving a sigh, I slump against the door. "Finally." Pushing off, I make my way back to my room and find Dean standing by my bed pulling his shirt on over his head. "Where are you going?"

He stops and turns to me, his eyes flat. Holding my gaze, he looks at me with complete disappointment and betrayal, causing my heart to drop into my stomach like lead. "I wouldn't have guessed if I didn't hear it for myself."

"Wh-what are you talking about, Dean?"

Shaking his head, he huffs a humorless laugh. "You're just like everyone else. Once a player, always a player, right?" I shake my head in denial as he continues, pointing a thumb at himself. "I'm the guy you want to brag to your friends that you fucked but you're too embarrassed to tell your family about."

"It's not like that!"

He steps towards me, staring into my eyes, his hurt and anger coming off him in waves. "It's not? Really Leah? Were you ever planning on telling Joe?" I flinch, not answering. He huffs another humorless laugh and shakes his head in disbelief.

"Dean…" I step towards him, but he flinches away from me the moment my hand skims his arm.

"Joe is one of my best friends. You think I would fuck around with you and risk losing a guy I consider a brother? There's very few people in my life I consider family, but you know Joe is one of them to me. You were *never* just another woman to me, but it's obvious the feeling is not mutual. I can't believe you of all people used me like everyone else. Fuck this!"

He steps around me, leaving me standing with my mouth open and tears streaming down my face. "I hope you got everything you wanted." The front door slams shut, the vibration shaking me.

My entire body trembles, consumed with guilt. What did I just do? I sink to the floor regretting everything I did and said in the last five minutes, but not sure if I can fix it.

Chapter 20

Dean

I stalk through my front door, my body tired from cleaning up around the property, but still vibrating with anger and betrayal, unable to rest. After taking a quick shower, I throw on jeans and a long-sleeved t-shirt. I need to find something else to do to get Leah out of my damn mind.

Grabbing my phone, I text Joe and Christian a message I'm sure they won't ignore. Confessing anything to Joe is stupid, but I do it anyway. "I'm fucked. I fell for the wrong woman and she screwed me over. I'm headed to Benny's. Join me for a drink?"

Ten minutes later I walk into the dimly lit bar, already flooded with twenty-somethings. I push my way to the bar, ordering a double shot of whiskey and whatever's on tap. I down the shot followed by the beer, immediately ordering myself another round. Grabbing the second shot, I tip my head back and swallow before he hands me the beer. I slide my card across the bar. "Start a tab?"

He nods, taking my card.

Just as I turn, a petite blonde steps in my path, fluttering her eyes at me. "Excuse me," I growl and step past her as if she's the blonde who scorned me.

I spot a booth in the back and make my way towards it as another woman calls my name. "Hey, Dean!" Not even bothering to turn my head, I lift my hand and flip her off, still walking.

"Holy shit, you're in fine form tonight," Joe mutters as he steps up behind me. "What the hell crawled up your ass?"

I slide into the booth, laughing manically and take another gulp of my beer as Joe slides in across from me holding a beer of his own. My eyebrows draw down in confusion. "How did you…"

He interrupts, "I was on the other side of the bar when you walked in. By the time I reached you, you downed a couple shots, a beer and pissed off two women. What the fuck is going on?"

"That's what I'd like to know," Christian mumbles as he slides in next to Joe. "That was one hell of a text."

"Yeah, but what else was I supposed to say to get you guys here?" They give each other a look before focusing back on me. "Let's just say I get it, Christian," I claim, taking another gulp of my beer.

"Get what?"

"I finally get why you were so fucked up when you lost Bree."

Christian runs his hand over his face and shakes his head. "Okay, but this shit didn't help and I became an asshole, someone who didn't deserve Bree."

"It doesn't matter, since she was just using me, does it? Who the fuck knows why, but she's just like everyone else. I thought her of all people would be different," I spit my words with venom.

"Why? Who is she?" Joe probes.

I shake my head. "Doesn't matter. I'm not good enough to share with anyone she cares about. Sleeping with a model apparently gives you bragging rights."

Joe's mouth drops open. "So, this girl slept with you because of the modeling thing I conned you into doing?"

Christian chuckles. "I heard about that. Way to step up, man. But if she's that shallow, she's not worth it."

I slam my fist down on the table, making both of them jump. "She is worth it!" Heaving a sigh, I mumble under my breath, "At least I thought she was."

The two of them look at each other and bring their gazes back to me. "Look," Joe starts, "maybe you just read her wrong."

I clench my fist, wanting to take a swing at my best friend. Christian, seeing my tension increase, raises his hand, attempting to calm me down. "Maybe whatever happened was a misunderstanding. If I know anything from experience, it's that things aren't always what they seem. If you've really fallen for this woman, fight for her. Don't follow my example, believe me, it will get you nowhere fast."

"Really?" I question, my disbelief apparent. After all, he's married to the love of his life. I down my beer and stand. "I'm going to get another beer. Want anything?" They shake their heads and I stalk towards the bar, focused on getting so drunk, I forget.

I find an open spot and order another beer and double shot, a woman cozying up to me on my right. "Want to buy me a drink?"

"Fuck, no." Her friend behind her laughs, but I ignore her. The next moment I catch sight of *her* walking in and freeze, her eyes widening the moment she spots me. The bartender slides the beer and the shot across the bar. "Can I have another one of these?" I hold up the shot. He pours it, sliding it over. Picking it up, I offer it to the woman who laughed when I shot her friend down.

She arches her eyebrows and shrugs, taking it from me.

We toast, downing the shot. Feeling Leah's eyes burning into the side of my head, my fingers twitch, wanting to hurt her like she did me. I step forward, pressing my lips to the woman in front of me, taking her by surprise, but she kisses me back. I tear my lips away from hers and grab my beer. "Thanks."

When I'm almost back to the table, I stumble over my feet at the sight of Leah and Scarlett, but they weren't invited to this party. "Fuck this." Grabbing a chair, I sit down at the end of the table. "Well, isn't this a *nice* surprise."

Joe gives me a look of warning, but fuck that. "Um, maybe we should go. We're supposed to meet up with Scar's friends anyway," Leah claims.

"They can wait." Scarlett waves her hand dismissively, a mischievous sparkle in her eye. "Where's the girl you were just making out with?"

"Which one?" My words hit their mark, Leah not able to hide her flinch. But it leaves me feeling empty. I glance at Christian and Joe; Christian narrowing his eyes on me while Joe watches his sister, his eyebrows drawn down in concern.

With a heavy sigh, I run my hand through my hair and drop it on the table feeling dejected. "You're right, Christian. I fucking hate it, but you're right." I shake my head and down my beer. "I gotta go."

Christian stands. "I'll give you a ride home."

I walk out, not bothering to say goodbye.

Chapter 21

Leah

Scar glances at me with a sad smile. "I'm going to get a drink. Want anything?" I'm too choked up to respond. "I'll surprise you."

The moment she walks away, I turn to my brother with tears streaming down my face. "Leah, what's wrong?" He slips into my side of the booth, wrapping me in a hug. "Who do I have to kill?"

"No." I shake my head, pushing away from my brother. "You're not doing anything. This is my fault. All my fault."

"What?" he questions his expression a look of both surprise and doubt.

Wiping away my tears, I insist, "I fucked up, Joe. I really fucked up and I don't know how to fix it."

"Talk to me. Tell me what's wrong. Maybe I can help."

I gulp down my nerves, glancing at my brother, my hand twisting together. "Just promise you'll listen before you say or do anything."

He gives me a look, his own suddenly more apprehensive. "You know I can't do that, but I promise I'll listen to everything you have to say, just please talk to me."

Sniffling, I nod, wiping my tears once again. My gaze shifts anxiously as I gather the courage to speak. "Okay. I'll try." Taking a deep breath, I exhale my confession, "I've had a crush on Dean since the first time you brought him home."

His eyebrows hit his hairline and his hand slams against the table making me jump. "I'll kill him."

"No!" I shake my head, grabbing onto my brother's arm and holding tight. "He didn't do anything wrong."

"If he hit on you, he sure as hell did!"

"It was me, just listen!"

Grimacing, he settles, grumbling his agreement, "Fine!"

Slowly, I release my hold on him, grateful when he doesn't move, continuing to watch me close. "He told me about his family, and about how people have always used him for his looks or his money, except for you and Christian and then I did and said something so stupid. I knew it would hurt him and I did it anyway. I hate myself for it."

"Leah, you're not making any sense. I know about people using him, but what the fuck does that have to do with you? What the hell did you do? Explain!"

"I'm trying. My head is just a mess."

"I'm sorry, I'm not trying to push you, but with what you've told me, nothing is making me less pissed at Dean. Just the opposite. I need more if you don't want me to do something stupid."

Nodding, I try to focus, knowing I need to admit more than I planned if I want this to come out right. "When you sent Dean to the photo shoot, that night a bunch of us went out for drinks."

"Okay and something happened with you two?"

I shake my head. "Not exactly. He saved me from that asshole you replaced."

"What do you mean saved you?" Joe's eyes widen and I quickly shake my head, trying to move past it.

"Nothing happened, but that's probably because Dean stopped him."

"Fuck, Leah!" He runs his hands through his hair in frustration.

"Anyway, he made sure I was safe the rest of the night and watched out for me after that. We started hanging out a lot too. And I really got to know him. At first, he said he couldn't go there with me because you're like a brother to him and he would never do that to you, but…" I trail off.

"But what?"

"I think he really had feelings for me, Joe, and I pretended like he was nothing." I wince, remembering my earlier words as my tears start to fall once again. "He got mad and left. He looked at me like I killed his puppy and laughed as he watched, but I just didn't want to get hurt. I was protecting myself and now he hates me."

"You and Dean?" he clarifies, his face pale.

"Yes, but…no, I don't think he'll ever forgive me and I wouldn't blame him." I sniffle, reaching for a napkin to wipe my nose.

Joe sighs heavily, running his hand through his hair. "When did this happen?"

"Yesterday morning."

He exhales harshly, muttering under his breath. "That explains why he's so fucked up. I've never seen him like this before." He groans, grasping the ends of his hair in frustration and tugging. "Fuck my life. You're right about one thing, Leah. I think he really did have feelings for you."

His words only make me cry harder. "Did?"

"Does…I mean I think he does have feelings for you. He wouldn't be this fucked up if he didn't give a shit about you."

"What am I going to do?"

"First, breathe. After, you calm down, you can still fix this, but really? Dean? You sure you really like him?"

"Yes!" I glare at my brother, wiping my tears away.

Eyes wide, he puts his hands up in surrender. "Okay, Okay. Just, relax. We'll figure it out. I promise."

"I hope so."

Scarlett returns, holding out a credit card. "I just closed the tab for your table on Dean's card."

My eyes widen. Scarlett just gave me a reason to show up at his door. Do I take it? Will he let me in if I do? Taking a deep breath, I muster my courage and reach for it, swiping it from her hand. "I'll bring it to him."

"Take it to him tomorrow," Joe suggests.

"Why?"

"He needs time to sober up so he remembers your conversation."

"That's probably a better idea anyway. I need to figure out what I'm going to say and hopefully he'll forgive me."

Chapter 22

Dean

My head feels like I lost in a boxing match, and my mouth tastes like I ate cotton balls doused in kerosene. I need to get up to get some aspirin and hydrate. I roll over, realizing too late I passed out on the couch and collide with the floor.

"Fuck!"

As I peel my eyes open, I groan, pushing myself off the floor, and stumble into the kitchen, straight for the aspirin. A knock at the door gives me pause and I brace myself against the counter, choking down the aspirin. Another knock. "I'm fucking coming!"

I yank open the door finding a wide-eyed Leah on the other side, looking gorgeous in black leggings, boots, and an oversized white sweater underneath her unzipped winter coat. "What the fuck are you doing here?"

She startles, but clenches her jaw, determined. "Can I come in?"

I push off the door frame and stalk towards the kitchen, grabbing a bottle of water, and returning to the couch. I chug the bottle, tossing it on the table before I lay down, closing my eyes.

The soft click of the door closing and tapping of her approaching footsteps, echoes like thunder in an approaching storm.

"Can you at least put a shirt on?"

Forcing my eyes open, I squint, looking down and realize I'm in nothing but boxers. I smirk, knowing there's no way in hell I'm moving an inch. "No."

"You left…"

"Can you talk a little quieter?"

Her voice softens. "You left your credit card with the bartender."

Prying my eyes open, I glance at her out of the corner of my eye, my card in her hand. "Thanks. You can leave it on the table."

She huffs. "You're not going to make this easy, are you?"

"Make what easy?"

"Dean…"

Shaking my head, I interrupt, "You used me. What the hell am I supposed to do with that?"

"I'm sorry."

I nod, her words hitting me hard. "Great. Now leave."

"No, I'm really sorry, Dean. I didn't mean what I said to Joe. I was just trying to protect myself after all the stories I've heard…"

I wince. "Yeah, stay away from the player."

"I don't think that of you."

"You sure?" I sit up wincing as I stare at her, clenching my jaw. "That's exactly who I used to be."

"But not anymore." I don't respond, but I don't have to. If she can't see that now–it doesn't matter anyway.

"Please." Her voice catches, making my chest tight. "I know I said some stupid things, but I didn't mean them. Please let me make it up to you."

I heave a sigh, running my hand through my hair. Can I let it go? Will she do anything different? How do I know? Tears spill over her lashes, squeezing my heart. "Fuck, please, don't cry, Leah. I can't handle seeing you cry."

"I'm sorry. Please forgive me," she insists, stepping closer.

The sincerity in her eyes appears genuine, but what does that mean to her? For us? "Why don't I get dressed and we can order some food and talk."

Her body sags in relief, making it feel as if an elephant is sitting on my chest. After everything, I need to be there for her, even if she doesn't want me the same way I want her. "Thanks."

"We need to figure out how we can…" pausing, I gulp hard before forcing out the rest, "be *friends*." The word taste like poison on my tongue. Yeah, nothing about this is going to be easy.

She flinches, piquing my curiosity, but after everything , I refuse to get my hopes up just to have my heart shredded once again.

Leah

"We need to figure out how we can…be friends." He gives me a look through narrowed eyes before he turns, trudging towards his room.

His words echo in my head, squeezing my heart. He wants to be friends? Jumping up, I follow him. "No!"

He pulls a t-shirt out of his dresser and tugs it over his head. "What?" he asks sounding exhausted.

"I don't want to be friends."

"You don't want to be friends?" His jaw ticks, his hands falling to his hips, drawing my attention to the deep V in his muscles below his belly button, just before his shirt falls the rest of the way, covering it. "What do you want?

"I want you to come to my parents' house on Christmas eve."

He shakes his head. "Tell Joe I'm good."

"It's not him asking, it's me."

He blanches. "No, thanks. I'm not coming to your house for Christmas out of guilt and pity. I'll be just fine on my own. I always am."

"It's not out of guilt or pity, Dean. I want you there! Please. I want you to come as my boyfriend."

He freezes. His eyes widen and he stares at me, his mouth falling slightly open. "Wait. What did you just say?"

I gulp down the lump in my throat. "I said, I want you to come to my parents' on Christmas Eve as my boyfriend. If that's what you want."

In an instant, he closes the distance between us, grasping my arms and staring into my eyes, begging for clarity. "Leah?"

"Dean, I've had a crush on you since the day I met you. I'm sorry for what I said, but I was afraid. I know it's no excuse, but I swear I didn't mean it. I'm crazy about you and I just want a chance."

He presses his lips to mine, my entire body sagging with relief as I melt into him, returning his kiss. He pulls back, the corners of his lips twitching up. "You've had a crush on me since you met me?"

My cheeks heat, but I nod, letting him relish in the moment. "You've always been hard for me not to notice."

He grins, his eyes sparkling. "Well, let's keep it that way." I giggle. "You know you're going to have to tell your brother. I'm not hiding anything from him, especially something like this; you and me." He presses a chaste kiss to my lips. "Us."

"That's not a problem because he, um, he already knows."

Deans eyes go wide. "What?"

"I was upset after you left and so when I talked to my brother and he told me you were at the bar, I wanted to see you. I was coming to apologize, but I saw you kissing someone else." My nose scrunches up and my stomach roils at the memory.

He winces. "Fuck, I'm sorry. When I saw you walk in–I only did that to piss you off. Childish, I know."

"It was my fault."

"No, you're not taking the blame for that. I can take credit for my stupid decisions. I'm sorry."

The candor in his eyes tightens my chest. "Thanks." Clearing my throat, I continue, "Anyway, when you left, I couldn't stop crying and I told Joe everything."

Arching his eyebrows he challenges, "Everything?"

My body heats and I shake my head. "Not everything. But I told him I liked you a lot and that I was the one who messed up. After my confession, he told me he thought you had real feelings for me. Is it true?"

He steps towards me and cradles my face in his hands. My heart beats rapidly, blood rushing in my ears. Taking a deep breath, I focus on the sound of his voice just to hear. "Fuck, yes."

I giggle, exhaling in relief. "Good."

"Leah, you make me feel alive. Your gorgeous, sexy, smart, driven." He brushes his lips over mine. "Your strength and courage are sexy as hell." His lips press against mine. "I've never met anyone like you." He moves his lips against mine. "But most of all, you make me feel like I'm home."

His words squeeze my heart in the palm of his hand. Needing to be close to him, I press my lips to his, and attempt to push my tongue inside, but he stops me. "You really don't want to do that. I might still be a little drunk. I need to eat something, drink some more water, and brush my teeth." He makes a face.

Laughing, I give him a chaste kiss. "Okay, I'll order us some food, while you brush your teeth."

"Deal."

"What are you hungry for?"

Ignoring my question, he wraps me in his arms once again, placing a kiss on the top of my head. "Thank you."

"For what?"

"For not giving up on me."

My heart clenches once again, making it difficult to breathe. "I'm the one who should be thanking you for giving me another chance."

He kisses the top of my head one more time as I melt into his embrace. I'm not sure how long we stand there before he finally slips away, my hopes for a future with him turning a corner.

Leah

Mindlessly, my fingers trail patterns on Dean's chest, a little in awe that I'm here and it's more than I ever imagined it could be. I press my lips to his side, a deep rumble coming from his chest. "Leah."

Lifting my head, I smile as his fingers run through my hair. "I like being able to kiss you anytime I want."

He grins. "You can do more than that."

I chuckle, my hand sliding down to his thick cock as my lips trail down his body. "More, like this?"

He moans. "That's not what I meant. You don't have to do that."

"I know." With wide eyes, I watch goosebumps erupt over his skin, loving that I'm the one getting this reaction out of him. Slipping my fingers into the waistband, I tug his boxers down, his dick springing free, already hard.

"Lee," he groans as I lick from base to tip. My tongue circles the end before sucking him into my mouth, hitting the back of my throat. "Fuck…" His hand tangles into my hair as I release him slowly and suck him in again and again, relishing his frenzied look as he starts to lose control.

Suddenly, he pops out of my mouth and I'm on my back, his lips pressed to mine, his tongue delving inside. I moan, my entire body tingling with anticipation… with need. He pulls back, breathless, yanking my shirt off in one swift movement. His lips fall back to my neck as his hand moves to my back, unclipping my bra and tossing it on the floor.

"I wasn't done," I claim, breathless.

"Later."

"Dean," I moan, my body curving into every touch, lick, kiss, needy for more. His hands roam my body, setting me on fire, my core burning for him.

His hand skims over my breasts, down my belly and into my pants, his fingers rubbing my clit and sinking deep into my pussy as I pant for breath.

"You're fucking soaked."

I don't respond, I can't. My leggings and underwear quickly disappear. "Please," I beg, barely breathing, "I want you, Dean."

He reaches over and I soon hear the crinkle of the wrapper as he rips open the condom, rolling it on. He hovers over me, kissing my lips, my jaw, my neck and back again. "Please, look at me."

Forcing my eyes open, I hold his intense gaze, feeling him at my entrance. "Please." I tug him towards me.

Granting my wish, he pushes slowly inside, my eyes rolling back in my head. My vision clears and I meet his stare. His expressive blue eyes reveal so much causing my heart to beat faster as he thrusts inside, slow, decisive, and possessive. My body arches, moving in sync with his. Everything about this feels different, my body and heart reacting as if claiming him as mine. Our breathing escalates as he attempts to maintain the torturously slow pace. But I can't take anymore.

I wrap my leg around his back, urging him on, moaning as he fills me up. Holding me tight, he kisses me, quickening our pace. With our bodies slick with sweat, he slides so deep, triggering something deep inside me. My insides tingle, burning, pulsing, the feeling intensifying, before I'm exploding, convulsing, and squeezing him tight, tipping him over the edge along with me.

"Leah," he groans, his movements erratic with my body milking him as we both ride out our high.

My body melts into the mattress, my limbs useless as he collapses by my side. He gets up, tossing the condom and returning to me with a sweet kiss, pulling me into his warm embrace. Sated and breathless, I smile, wondering how I got so lucky, but grateful he's really mine.

My heart feels full as I look at Dean, knowing I'm without a doubt falling in love with him, but I can't tell him–yet. I don't think he's ready to hear it. I've always known if I ever had this chance with him, he would be the one man I would never be able to let go.

Knowing that chance is truly within grasp, his forgiveness, and this opportunity to be with him is all I ask. The possibility of us consuming all my senses.

I feel him kiss the top of my head once again before he speaks. "I think we need to keep working on you making it up to me. I'll be ready to go again in a few minutes."

I chuckle and press my lips to his chest. "I'm in."

Chapter 25

Dean

My heart thrashes against my ribcage as I stare at the familiar front door. Why the fuck am I nervous? This is Joe's house. Leah's. I've been here so many times, although, neither of them actually live here anymore…

The door swings open and I lift my gaze. Leah stands in front of me looking stunning in a red, scoop-neck dress, trimmed with black velvet, hugging her curves in all the right places. "You look gorgeous."

"Thank you, so do you." She pushes her blonde hair behind her ear and smiles. "I saw you through the window."

Knowing she caught me fighting with myself, I shrug, offering her a crooked smile. "I like the cold."

"Apparently." She laughs, holding her hand out for me. I take it. Instantly, my body calms as she tugs me inside. "Merry Christmas." Pushing up on her tiptoes, she presses her lips to mine.

"Merry Christmas." I grin.

"Damn. I just can't get used to this," Joe grumbles as he walks into the foyer, clenching his jaw.

Grinning, I kiss her again before looking at my best friend. "Figure it out. I'm not going anywhere."

He smiles. "Good." I step back from Leah and he gives me a one-armed hug with a hard pat on the back, reiterating, "Don't fuck this up."

Grabbing his shoulder, I move back slightly and hold his gaze, needing him to know my truth. "I won't."

Giving me a firm nod, he returns my intense gaze and grins. "I know. Merry Christmas, brother."

Brother. The single word slams into me like a freight train. If Leah decides to marry me one day, Joe would really be my brother. I gulp down the lump in my throat and blink back the sudden onslaught of emotions. This isn't something I'm used to. "Merry Christmas, Brother." My voice cracks and I clear my throat, stepping back. "Is there somewhere I can put these?" I hold up a bag filled with Christmas presents.

"Let's put them under the tree in the family room," Leah suggests, her own eyes watery. I follow, finding the room filled with their family; their mom, dad, aunts, uncles, cousins, and grandparents.

A chorus of, "Merry Christmas," sounds from around the room, overwhelming me yet again.

I smile, each of them greeting me with a hug, while Leah puts the presents under the tree.

"It's Mister December 5th!" Her grandmother cheers making me blush, Leah giggle and Joe groan.

"We love seeing you and Leah together. She's so happy," her mom gushes. "We were thrilled when she asked if she could bring her new boyfriend with her and knowing it's you–" she claps her hands in excitement and continues, "Well, we're just happy that you two are together."

I glance at Leah, enjoying her deep blush. "Mom…" she warns, entwining my fingers with hers.

The chatter, the banter, the laughter, and the love remain prominent as the night continues making my heart feel full. Because of Leah, the missing pieces of my life are falling into place. The way she holds my heart like a treasure; like I'm worth it is everything and yet she has no idea what she does to me. I look down at her, my chest tight.

She meets my gaze. "Dean?"

Not able to hold it in another moment, I blurt out the words I know with everything in me. "I love you, Leah." Her eyes widen, a soft gasp escaping her lips as I pull her into my arms. "I don't expect you to say it back, but I need you to know I'm so in love with you. You have given me the world by just being you and I will work my ass off to be the Saint Nick you deserve every single day."

She laughs. I silence her with a sweet kiss, our heads coming together as our lips part. "I love you, too, Dean." Her words fill me up, my heart feeling like it's about to explode. I never imagined it could feel this way. This is a first for me and I'm never letting the feeling go or the beautiful woman in my arms. "And don't you know by now? You've already given me everything I've ever wanted."

"Merry Christmas, Lee."

The End

Other Books by Nikki A Lamers

<u>The Unforgettable Series</u>
<u>Unforgettable Summer</u>
<u>Unforgettable Nights</u>
<u>Unforgettable Dreams</u>
<u>Unforgettable Memories</u>
<u>Unforgettable One</u>
<u>Unforgettable Mistakes</u>

<u>Mending Shattered Hearts Series</u>
<u>Breaking Cycles</u>
Breaking Barriers (Coming Soon)

<u>The Home Series</u>
<u>Dreams Lost and Found</u>
<u>Finding Home</u>

<u>Piper Falls: Station 28</u>
<u>Leave of My Duty</u>

Connect with the Author

Official Author Website
www.nikkialamersauthor.com

Linktree for All Author Links
https://linktr.ee/NikkiALamersauthor

<u>*Acknowledgements*</u>

As always, thank you to the most important people in my world, my family, Michael, Tyler, Allison, and our dogs, and my mom, my dad in heaven and my sister, as well as my extended family. I appreciate your constant love and support more than anything! I wouldn't be able to do what I love without you.

Thank you to those that started the journey of this book with me with the limited time anthology, Jingle Balls including Annie Mick, Kayla Baker, Melony Ann, and Samantha Michaels. The story has changed since the release of that book and I hope you enjoy the updated version. Thank you to Nick and Carxander Publishing for all your help!

Thank you to Dina Huesseini for editing the original and Darley Collins for always being there for feedback! I truly appreciate you both!

To all my fellow author friends, I'm incredibly grateful for every one of you. You are all fantastic writers, supporters, and friends! I'm thankful for all of you keeping me sane, providing help and encouragement and cheering louder than I thought possible! I love writing and being able to share it with all of you!

I hope we all can continue to read, share, and enjoy! Thank you!

About the Author

Award Winning Author, Nikki A Lamers grew up in Wisconsin and lived in Florida for a few years before ending up on Long Island in New York where she now lives with her husband and their two teens. She writes mostly spicy contemporary and new adult romance, many times incorporating tough health, wellness, and life issues. With her public health background, she loves diving deep into her characters and seeing how some of the tough issues can impact an individual and their relationships. Recently she has expanded her writing with romantic suspense, romantasy and paranormal romance, while maintaining her roots. Writing, reading, coffee, chocolate, and at times a good drink are all she wants alongside her friends and family. Since meeting her husband, they enjoy spending time in Maine and exploring different places, meeting new people, and always crafting her next story. For her other job she freelances as a script writer, advisor, and supervisor on and off set, hoping to one day see a story of her own on screen.